Jonathan Ames'
I PASS LIKE NIGHT

"This is New York at street level. Ames is something of a gambler [but he] negotiates the pitfalls with remarkable dexterity.... There is an unforced sadness at the heart of this novel, and there lies the proof that the gamble has succeeded."

—*The Times Literary Supplement* (London)

"Unerringly builds up an accurate portrait of a dissolute young man floundering in a sea of amorality."

—*Time Out*

"Ames' stoic tone does not mask the cry in his voice. Each short passage captures a concise, poignant moment whose pain Ames drives home....a timely tale."

—*Minneapolis Daily*

I PASS LIKE
NIGHT

I PASS LIKE NIGHT

JONATHAN AMES

VINTAGE CONTEMPORARIES

VINTAGE BOOKS

A DIVISION OF RANDOM HOUSE, INC. NEW YORK

First Vintage Contemporaries Edition, August 1990

Copyright © 1989 by Jonathan Ames

All rights reserved under International and Pan-American Copyright
Conventions. Published in the United States by Vintage Books, a division
of Random House, Inc., New York. Originally published by
William Morrow and Company, Inc., in 1989.

Library of Congress Cataloging-in-Publication Data

Ames, Jonathan.
I pass like night / Jonathan Ames.
p.   cm.
Reprint. Originally published: New York : W. Morrow, c1989.
ISBN 0-679-72857-0 (pbk.)
I. Title.
PS3551.M42I16   1990
813'.54—dc20   89-40502
CIP

Manufactured in the United States of America
10 9 8 7 6 5 4 3 2 1

To Jim Stevenson

Heaven lies about us in our infancy!
Shades of the prison-house begin to close
Upon the growing Boy

—WILLIAM WORDSWORTH
"Ode: Intimations of Immortality"

I PASS LIKE
NIGHT

GOLDIE

    I like this one whore on the lower East Side, her name is Goldie because of her teeth, and she's really sweet. She's a big black woman with big breasts and I saw her for the first time a few nights ago when it was too hot to sleep. I came out of my room around one A.M. and I walked down to Grand and she was there. She was wearing a black bra like a bikini and a tight black miniskirt and black high heels. I went past her slow and my eyes ran over her breasts and down her stomach and she smiled at me and she took the plastic straw out of her mouth that she was chewing on and she said real nice, "Ya goin' out honey?" And I said, "Yeahhh," real hesitant and shy and embarrassed like it was my first time, but I knew what we were going to do, and I came down there to do it, "I . . . I am."

    "Well, come here honey, follow me."

    So she took my hand and led me across the street.

She took me into the old dark park with its broken fences, crumbling walls, and shadows that smell of piss and garbage and thrown away condoms.

"You wanna fuck or you wanna suck?"

I said fuck, real quiet and sweet in a whisper, and she said, "O.K., honey, I'll just bend over and you stick it right in." And that's what I wanted, to be lost in the great black ass of this great black woman twice my size. Lost in some hole I'm scared of, lost in the dark hole between her legs, my little white body, hips half the size of hers—pulled in, sucked in, and lost forever. But she said, "That's gonna cost forty-five." And my great dream was crushed, and I was back in the park, back in reality, and I said, "I only got twenty." Which was stupid, because I knew I'd have to settle for a blow job, and once you tell a whore how much money you got you have to give them the whole thing. At least I do, because in a half-crazy way I'm scared of whores and I'd rather pay than get in a fight with one. Although if I had told her I only had ten dollars she would have given me a blow job just the same.

But Goldie was special, I almost feel as if I could trust her. She said, "No girl out here let you fuck for twenty, but I'll give you a blow job and let you play with my tits too." Now, she's out there like all the other whores to make some bucks, but she also wants to give you your money's worth. Not too many whores on the street are like that.

She asked for the twenty and I gave it to her,

you always pay before things get started. She put the bill in her little purse and she dug around in there for a condom. I pulled my pants and underwear down and she said, "What's your name?" All the whores ask that, and I don't know why, maybe it's to make you feel comfortable, so usually I lie, but this time I didn't, I liked her, I said, "Alexander." She smiled and said, "I'm Goldie," and in the dark I could see her teeth.

She got the condom out and I felt a little embarrassed that I had pulled down my pants and underwear myself. I still wanted to play the game that I had no idea what was happening. I almost expected her to be surprised that my pants were down, but she didn't seem to notice. She put her hand on me to get me ready, but I was already hard, and she made a little whistling sound to make me feel good. She knelt down and rolled the dry condom on me— whores use cheap ones that aren't lubricated. She said, "I gotta use the condom, honey, so nobody gets no germs." That was fine with me and she started sucking and I leaned back against the park wall and put my hand down her neck and into the tight crack between her moist, big, beautiful breasts.

We were hidden in the sunken part of the park, which must have been a children's playground once. Above the wall I leaned against was a row of old dark trees, a low iron fence, and some benches. On one of the benches off to the left I could make out two men sitting and watching Goldie give me a blow job. I figured they were old Bowery bums drinking or young kids shooting heroin. They probably sat there all night and watched a hundred guys drop their pants for the whores. Maybe more, I don't know. I've often wondered how many men street whores go with in a night. All those penises in their mouths and rotten, hairy crotches in their faces. That's why they suck on you like a machine, up and down they go as fast as they can. They open their mouths wide, then jab their heads back and forth like a piston, with the penis going all the way to the back of their throats. They want you to come as quick as possible so they can get back out on the street and make more money. The pleasure is not that great, at least not for me anyways.

Sometimes though something strange can happen, like being with Goldie. She was busy sucking away and I was busy with her tits, when suddenly she stopped, looked up at me, and said, "Come on baby, come for Mama!" That sounded good to me and gave me a little extra jolt, and they're always trying to rush you, but Goldie was nice about it, so I was about to come for her, to please her, when another whore appeared in the opening of the sunken area and whispered in a raspy, warning voice, "SQUAD, and they gonna do somethin', I can feel it." Goldie stood up, gave a quick look to the street, took her purse off the top of the wall, and told me, "Duck down, honey, there's a squad out there." She ducked down too, but made sure to hold on to my cock so it wouldn't go soft. I looked through the opening of the park and saw the police car at the corner about fifty yards away. I looked at Goldie and she was giving me an occasional quick suck and keeping her eye on the street at the same time. The car just lingered there and the whores were quiet, still, and waiting. Finally, the cops pulled away and the other whore said, "They gone, but they gonna come back."

I suddenly had incredible respect for these whores. In my mind I likened them to the great jungle cats of the Tarzan books I had read when I was young. These cats, Numa the lion and Sheeta the leopard, knew every creature that passed through the forest and knew what it would do. More whores came to hide in the park and they were all like those cats, hissing to one another "ssquad . . . sssquad . . . they comin'." I just kept my head below the wall and leaned back with my knees bent while Goldie sucked even more furious than before. I waited for the cops' spotlight to land on me and I wondered if they handcuffed prostitutes' johns and I almost hoped that they would come so I could run, so that my childhood games of escape from prison could come true.

They passed by again, but this time they didn't stop. They seemed to be stalking us, circling around the park, coming down Chrystie Street, then going up Forsythe. Under the streetlights I could see the car so clearly, as if it was the first police car I had ever seen. In my eyes it was almost beautiful, with its tubed, red roof light and the driver's blue arm hanging out the window. One of the whores said, "They only bluffin', they know we're in here and they gonna bring us all in, you better hurry up Goldie and get rid of your boyfriend." I knew I had better come soon or I wouldn't come at all, and I didn't want to waste the twenty bucks. But with all the excitement I had become distracted and Goldie could tell, so between sucks she started urging me, "Come on honey give me your juice . . . I want all of it baby . . . shoot it baby . . . shoot it!"

The other whores started laughing. Laughing at me. One of the whores said, "Tell 'em how to do it, Goldie, tell that boy how." And Goldie kept on saying, "Shoot it!" and they kept on laughing. I sort of wished that Goldie would say, "Do it for Mama," it had excited me a little before, and then maybe I could come, but I was too embarrassed to ask. So I tried to concentrate. I kept my dick in her mouth, my hand on her breasts, and my eyes on the street for the police.

Finally, I willed myself to come, although I barely felt it. She noticed a change in me, the end of the slight swaying of my hips.

"Did you come, honey?"

"Yes, I did."

"You sure?" She looked at me with concern. "Weeze gotta make sure you come, you been so nice."

"It's O.K., I'm fine."

"All right, goodnight, honey."

She walked away sexy and proud and the other whores left too. My pants were at my knees, the police hadn't come back, and I peeled the condom off my dick. It pulled on the hairs, and I hate that, and it was wet with her saliva. When I got it off I tossed it to the ground and tried to give a confident nod of my head to the guys on the bench in case they were looking. I pulled my pants up and I cut the opposite way from the whores through the long, dangerous park with shadows jumping at me from the corners my eyes.

I was running quick over the choppy pavement and broken glass and I leaped up part of the wall, and as I jumped I had a moment of elation. I was elated because Goldie was a good whore and let me touch her tits. I was elated because I was passing through a park "no one should walk through." And I was elated because I heard the other whores say squad and because they laughed at me.

I ran all the way back to my building and when I got to my metal door the cops cruised by and I looked to the corner, but Goldie wasn't there. She was a smart one and I was safe too and I climbed up the dirty stairs to my summer hot room and I went to the toilet. I took a long piss and I was glad because I always want to believe that if you piss after sex with a whore you won't get a disease. But then I looked at my penis and it was all red and abused looking. There was even a bit of ripped condom sticking to it. I wondered if it had ripped while she was sucking me, and I wondered if it did if a little bit of disease, all it takes, made it through that little rip and made contact with a little bit of me. I peeled off that piece of shredded condom and washed my dick, then dried it with a paper towel. I looked at myself in the mirror, at my red eyes and greasy nose. And I thought to myself, the most sobering thing in the world is to look in the mirror and see how ugly you really are.

ALL I KNOW is myself. I was born twenty years after the end of the war. My father around the time of my birth was very good looking with short black hair. My mother was a radiant blonde and I was her love. She often says to me now: "You were such a gentle baby, I used to look forward to you getting up. Most mothers want their babies to sleep." Usually I like it when she says that, I love flattery of any sort even if it's about a me and time I don't even know. But sometimes she says it with such a sigh, that I ask in my mind, "aren't I a love now mom?" She would answer, "Of course you are, if anything happened to you my life would be over, I love you." But I don't ask.

A PORTRAIT OF
A FATHER

My father gave me ten dollars when I went home and he said: "I wish I had somebody to give me ten dollars." He's still looking for somebody to take care of him, he did what he was told, but it didn't work out, so he's looking for a savior, and he wants me, his son, to be his father. And I love him, I look at him from far away sometimes like at temple when he's at the torah in front of the congregation and I'm sad suddenly to see how old he's become, I haven't really looked at him in so long. But then I'm proud to watch him make his faces and say his prayers, and I wonder if anyone in the congregation will remember Ira Vine as he stood there or do they not see him, as I haven't for so long. Who is that man up there that I want to say "I love you" to and how good that would make him feel, he's failed in everything else, but if he could be confident in his son's love . . . I know he tries to be strong for me, on the phone to New York he'll say, "Goodnight, son." And just from those two words I hear him trying, trying to be a father, saying son.

But then he comes back down from the torah and he's up close again, and the burden is too great for me to comfort him with my pride and love for him, and somehow it turns to the old repulsion. For years as a child I couldn't bear to watch him eat, I would move as far away into the corner of the table, it wasn't a big table, and I'd turn my head, I couldn't stand the sounds he made. And he would make me scratch his back, his hairy back, and somehow it was a test of my love if I didn't scratch hard enough, but I was horrified to get things under my fingernails and he didn't understand that. And he would take baths with my sister and myself, and he always wanted to cuddle, and I remember feeling his penis against the crack of my ass, and who knows what that has done to me.

And all I've heard for the last ten years is his crying and weeping, about how he would be better off dead, and his heart palpitations and anxiety attacks and a problem with his shoulder, hand, knee, wrist, eyes, What's bothering you today, Dad? He's a Depression-born child and all the values he had don't work, and he was a momma's boy because he had a hole in his ear, IRA DON'T GO SWIMMING, DON'T GET YOUR HEAD WET, IRA YOU HAVE TO GO TO THE DOCTOR. His mother, my grandmother, who babied him for a long time, died two years ago. (His father, long dead, never encouraged him, only told him, "Promise me you won't be a taxi driver," since he had been a taxi driver in Brooklyn during the Depression. So my father kept the promise and became a traveling salesman in the northeast corridor.) So now that his momma is dead, my father is more lost than ever—he has no one's expectation not to live up to anymore ("Why are you a salesman? Why couldn't you have been something?" she would say well into his fifties.) But he doesn't realize how freeing her death is, he still looks in the mirror and hears her saying "failure." So he takes naps all the time and doesn't feel well. Every time I've eaten at home the last ten years he starts the meal by saying, "I don't feel right," and one time I jumped up and screamed, "Dad, this is serious," so I dialed 911. My mother laughed with me. And even he smiled. He hasn't felt right for a decade.

I asked him once, "Dad, what were your dreams?" I was trying to figure out why he had been depressed for so long, and he said, "To marry your mother, have you kids, have a house, a car, and a dog." So I said, "What's the problem then? You've got everything." He just shook his head, somehow it isn't enough and he has no new dreams. He just keeps his job because he is afraid to quit, and afraid to lose his company car, he hasn't paid for his own gas in years. As a traveling salesman, he can tell you the year of a photograph if his car is in the background; he's had over twenty-five company cars since the fifties and he remembers each one. Sometimes I try to think of him as a brave knight of the roads traveling eight hundred miles a week to factories in East Stroudsburg and Gloversville to sell tool and die. And over the years he's learned all the roads without tolls and what number to order at Howard Johnson restaurants, and how to make his brakes last an extra ten thousand miles. He never stopped being a good father though, he'd bathe me and bring me juice at night and miss work to help my mother take care of me when I was sick. But he's defeated now, too many miles on roads through the Poconos dark and winding and his eyes burning from his own cigar smoke and fatigue, and one thing kept him from driving off the road, and that's his great love for my mother.

So now he is terrorized by his two young Jewish bosses, the Feldmans, who grow fantastically in size and evilness every year. I tell him, "Dad, stop worrying, they like you, it's all in your mind." And sure enough, they said, "Ira, we wouldn't hurt a Jewish boy." And he's fifteen years older than they are. And he fears they'll find the extra two hundred dollars a year worth of gas he puts in my mother's car. Now towards the end of his career they've struck him the greatest salesman's blow, after twelve years on salary they've put him on commission, to light a fire under his sixty-year-old ass.

And he's had one outlet over the years from his job as a salesman, and that outlet was guns. For a while he even rode in auxiliary police cars, he loved the uniform, but then the governor made it illegal for volunteers to carry guns (some volunteer shot somebody without warning). So now he just lies in front of the TV on a couch with a blanket wrapped around him, and our dog lying between his legs, and out of that blanket sticks his gun and he dry fires it at the TV, aiming between the eyes.

I WAS WALKING up Chrystie Street to get to Second Ave. and a bum on a bench sitting straight and proud and crazy with all his plastic bags about him, waved a great stick, and shouted to me through his wiry beard, "I have a fourteen-inch cock and twenty-three grandchildren throughout the whole world!"

I said, wrongly thinking that I could communicate with all the street people of New York, "With a cock like that you should have a hundred grandchildren."

"You're a good friend," he said softly, then he changed his tone so wildly and unexpectedly and screamed in a deep voice, "so get the fuck out of here before I break your neck!" I played the New York game and just went on walking, acting cool; just in case though I counted ten steps, and turned around real fast. I didn't want to get killed by some mad rasputin bum attacking from behind.

DOORMAN

I'm the number-two doorman of The Four Seasons restaurant. I'm like the second guy the manager pulls out of the bullpen in the ninth, but that doesn't mean I'm not effective. I work Monday, Tuesday, and Wednesday nights, and Dimitri the seventeen-year veteran ace of the staff gets the big games, the big crowds on Thursday, Friday, and Saturday. Sometimes I fill in for him or I do a special errand like drive the owner home, but generally those three nights of work fill my pockets with enough cash to pay for my room, my food, and the few extra pleasantries I like to spoil myself with. Some people call the extra change cigarette money, but I don't smoke.

Being a doorman the way I like to do it means you hustle all the time. The entrance to The Four Seasons is in the middle of Fifty-second and since it's a cross street it's hard to hail a cab, so I run up fast to Park Avenue and blow my whistle there. The traffic on the avenue is thick with taxis and the drivers hear my call and spot my summer-pink doorman's hat (green in the spring, red in the fall, brown in the winter), they know I'm the Four Seasons man and they pull into the top of Fifty-second. I hop into the back seat of their taxi and I always say, "Thanks man, down to the canopy." It makes me happy to connect with other working men and bring them business, and we fly the half block to the restaurant's entrance and I spring out. My customers are always surprised to see me, because I greet them at the door and then I vanish up the block, out of their sight until I appear again majestically out of the back seat of a yellow, holding the door open with a flourish, tipping my hat, bowing slightly, and saying, "Here's your taxi, sir," and they palm me a dollar and I take the bill, tip my hat again, and put the money in my pocket as smooth as breathing. I slam the door shut, the cab is gone, another pulls up and takes its place, I open the door and the fancy people don't see me, I say, "Welcome to The Four Seasons," and I slide to the restaurant's portal and it's open before they know it, I give a little bow, usually no tip on the way in but sometimes there is, so I'm always on the ham. Another couple comes out of the restaurant while I still hold the door, I say, "Would you like a taxi, sir?" and he nods yes, and I'm running again, to Park Avenue, blowing my whistle, catching a cab.

I work hard to make my tips, I can clear a hundred a night, and some of the people are regulars and they give me the keys to their Mercedeses when they park illegally, so I can move them if necessary and I'm not supposed to do that, but they slip me a ten or a five and I act very polite. Dimitri trained me for a few nights in the beginning and he never said it out loud, he almost never speaks, but I learned how you let a few regulars think that they're the Daddy Warbucks of your blue-collar life and they'll slip you a nice tip just for standing there and taking in air. I'm getting pretty good at that, but my big dream is that one day I'll open a limo door and lock eyes with a rich woman widow with large breasts and a string of pearls around her neck. I'm hoping for this electric moment when she knows I'm the boy she's been looking for and she gives me a card with a number and no name, and walks in the restaurant like I'm not even there, because the whole thing has got to be secret from the start. If my mind really takes off I start projecting down the road a few months and I see black-and-white pictures of myself in Vanity Fair, cozying up next to her in a crushed-red-leather booth wearing a black tie and holding my hand in front of our faces. It's something to keep me going when I'm opening doors all night long and if I'm not thinking about that, then I'm usually keeping an eye open for the celebrities who like the Four Seasons cuisine. For the most part it doesn't thrill me, but I like to be able to spot them, it's a hobby, and it makes me feel good about the restaurant, to know that I'm working at a classy place. And when the State Department stars show up I like talking with the Secret Service agents and looking for the gun bulge under their jackets and the one above their ankles. So generally the celebrity thing doesn't throw me too much, except one time the Orioles' shortstop showed up for dinner. I'm a personal fan of his and he's the only celebrity that I've come close to asking for an autograph from. But at the time I remembered that he was in a slump and I didn't want to disturb him.

Like in every profession there's lots of little lessons and rules of etiquette like that and I'm proud at how I've developed a doorman's instincts for all aspects of this job. Just yesterday afternoon a single, good looking woman in her mid-thirties in an expensive dress that looked cheap went in around five o'clock. Our eyes caught for a second and there was that extra bit of communication and our brains talked without our lips moving and I knew what she was and she knew what I was too. The restaurant has a bar, but it's not the kind of place to free lance, so I was getting my first look at an Upper East Side lady at work, it must have been a scheduled date. Sure enough a half hour later she came out with a man in a very fine suit and I said, "Would you like a taxi, sir?" He said yes, and I got one fast and held the door open. He paused a second before getting in and I looked at his hair, it was very thin (I'm always looking at men's hair wondering how my own scalp will be decimated), and he said to the woman quick in a whisper so he would know what to tell the taxi driver, "Where do you want to go, The Plaza? The Pierre?" She said, "Your wish is my command," and there was a paid for smile on her face that got me excited. They went in the taxi and the man forgot to tip me, but this was one time I didn't mind. I closed the door gently.

I went back to the canopy smiling and a couple of the limo drivers were out of their cars leaning against the Seagram's building smoking and talking. They knew what had gone down and this one ex-cop who had driven for the man said, "See how I turned my head when he came out, I act like I don't know him, no eye contact, no nothing. That's being sharp. I might have to drive him and his wife next week, you never know, so it's none of my business if he's playing around with whores behind his wife's back. You got to show respect, if you gotta be blind you gotta be blind." The other limo drivers agreed and I thought it was pretty sound and after that the rest of the night went along pretty smooth and un-eventful.

I took my half-hour dinner break which is one of the chief benefits of the job. Every night, like last night, I go through the first dining room. The twenty-foot rows of beaded metal oscillate and glimmer and cover the giant tinted-glass fronts. I look at all the people dining in the rich brown leather light and yellow candle glow, every night is like a Broadway opening, the Maître D' sprays his hair, and all the wealthy people look clean and from a distance they make it look pretty to eat. I go into the steaming kitchen and I know how to move my body in the hectic rush of waiters and busboys; and the fourteen stoic cooks sweat over their fires and one man shouts orders into a microphone in a coded language and I always say thank you for my meal. Usually one of the waiters who likes me will spot me and cut me a slice of one of the desserts, and a pro will always take time to do something like that because even when you're paid you always feel like you're giving too much, so a stolen piece of pie brings something back, helps to tip the scales, and I always eat it even if I don't want to.

After dinner last night my favorite waiter gave me a slice of the house specialty, Chocolate Velvet, and then I worked hard until two A.M., an hour later than usual because there was a private party. I was on the job almost ten hours and my knees and feet hurt from all the running and standing, and my mouth muscles ached from blowing my whistle and sometimes I get nervous thinking about permanent mouth damage. But last night, like so many nights, I love it when it's late and my shift is almost over, and Park Avenue is still and dead, and I'm all alone and small at the corner of so many great buildings. I've seen the day's traffic flood pass and the avenue is an empty bed now and maybe because rich people live here it always seems to glisten, and I blow my whistle into New York and some taxi driver somewhere with his window open, feeling like I do, will hear my plea and he'll come running, and I'll have another buck tip in my pocket.

31

MY FRIEND, THE GENTLEMAN SHOPPER

I have this friend who every couple of months calls me up around two A.M. and says, "Alexander, do you want to go shopping?" He says it like that to hide what he really means, which is: "Alexander, do you want to come with me and search for the whores who line the dark side streets near the Lincoln Tunnel?" He's usually embarrassed when he makes these calls, because after every time we do it he swears that he will never go with a whore again. But every couple of months the phone rings late at night and I know it's him. He can't stay away, he loves the thrill of shopping too much. He says that with all the whores on the street that he feels like he's in a candy store or toy department of women. And he is very kind to the whores he carefully chooses and likes to make small talk and offer them tissues to wipe their mouths after they're done. I know he does that because I've been in the back seat and he's even offered tissues to my whores.

One time when we went out, before they started using condoms, his whore wagged her head no to the offer of the tissue and instead leaned across him and spit his sperm out his open window. She got out of the car and he sat there in shock. I couldn't think of anything to say to comfort him and after a while we drove away. I turned around, looked out the back window, and saw a truck pass over the splotch in the road that was his sperm. I thought of it being in the tire's tread and being carried far out into New Jersey and beyond, spread over highways everywhere, his DNA merging with the dashed lines of the Jersey Turnpike.

I CAME OUT of the subway and saw a bum on his elbows and knees in the Spring Street park. He was crawling on the asphalt, choking and heaving. He had no shirt on and he had a broad hairy back like my father and I could see his ribs poking through his skin like the carcass of a dead cow. And his face was all bashed in, swollen scabs where his eyebrows used to be, from drunken falls down steps or kicks to the face while sleeping. He had no shoes and his feet from dirt were like burned stubs at the ends of his legs. I held on to the chain fence, like a prison fence, and watched him through its little squares.

J.B. came alongside me and said, "How ya doing, Red?" I turned and smiled at him, he is one of the oldest bums on the street and my favorite because he has blue eyes like my Grandfather did. "I'm O.K., J.B., but who's that guy?" I pointed to the bum in the park. J.B. answered, shaking his head, "That poor fella is Mike McDonnel, he used to ride around here in a great big Buick and give some of the boys jobs; you shoulda seen 'em then, musta weighed 250 pounds and smoked cigars, he'd help somebody out back then if he could. The fellas would crowd around his Buick. 'Mike, you gotta little work for me? Hey Mike, can you a spare five?' But what good is it anyways? Look at him, he's one of us now."

RAINSTORM

This summer was gruesomely hot and at one point it hadn't rained for weeks. New York was surrounded by prison walls of its own thick, unmoving moisture, until one night, thankfully, the skies could hold no more and the flood gates were opened. Now normally I don't like to get soaked by New York rain, I figure I'll go blind or my eyebrows will fall out, but this downpour had me especially frightened. During these last few weeks the clouds had been storing up poisons like an alcoholic's liver, and I didn't want to be caught underneath it now that it had been sliced open. So even though I was only a few blocks from my apartment, I dashed nervously into this new bar on East Third Street. It's all white inside, very pure and very clean, and that night the place was empty except for a few people at one of the tables. I was the only one at the bar and that's when I met Joy, she was the bartender. I ordered a beer and wiped the water off my hands, face, and hair with several napkins. I made quite a little pile of them and calmed my nerves by sipping my beer. It was coming down so thick that I could barely see the street outside. I had visions of people drowning in the avenues and was a little concerned to be on the ground floor, but the door seemed to be well sealed. Joy smiled at me, she sensed my nervousness about the rain, and I sensed her boredom, the place was practically empty, so we started talking.

She went into a monologue telling me her life story, about her career as an uncommissioned sculptor and I was supplying a few well timed grunts and "I know what you mean's" and "Is that so's," but I was really only half listening. I was too busy being attracted to her. She has a pretty face, a little pale but that's to be expected in New York, with pouty lips, a fine straight nose, and short, chestnut brown hair. She was wearing a baggy, sleeveless, V-neck blouse, and though she was very thin, I would get flashes of very deep, very dark, well defined armpits, which intrigued me to no end. She was a bit strange what with talking fast and her hand trembling as she lifted her cigarette, but already I was thinking about seeing her nude. I like to see them nude first a couple of times and try to get things straight before all the confusion begins.

So there I was in a fairly pleasant, slightly tense state alternating between my happy erotic thoughts about her mysterious armpits and being nervous that her waving cigarette would light the now dry napkins, which were still piled in front of me, into a small pyre; when she finally said something that piqued my interest.

". . . When my lawsuit comes through and I get my money, I'm getting the hell out of New York and buying a home in Vermont. Did you know there are no pollutive factories in Vermont?"

I didn't answer her last question, I was excited by the idea of a lawsuit and money. "You have a lawsuit? Against who?"

"Dalkon Shield." She said that with a certain pride and satisfaction.

"What's Dalkon Shield?"

"You never heard of it?"

"No, what is it?" I thought it sounded vaguely like a household poison product I had seen advertised on TV.

"It's an IUD, you know, birth control. You sure you haven't read about it or something? It was on *60 Minutes* a couple of years ago."

"I've heard of girls dying from their tampons."

"That's sort of the same thing. Some women did die and their families are the top cases, the ones with the most damage to claim. I'm near the top, but I've been waiting nine years for a settlement. Nine years. Can you believe it? I just want what I deserve, you know? But everyone who ever used the thing is jumping on the bandwagon and trying to get money out of it, even if nothing happened to them. They're slowing the whole thing down for the people who are really hurt, like me. And can you imagine the families of the dead girls waiting nine years?"

She put out her cigarette as a dramatic finish to her question and I sipped my beer. She went to help the people at the table who were calling her over and I looked at the cigarette in the ashtray. I thought of my father telling me about a crazy (*meshugga*) Rabbi who put out his cigarettes and then with great concentration cut up the butts in thirds with his sharpened thumb nail. My father said, "You could tell he was sick by the way he put out his cigarette." Since then I've always checked to see if anybody did that, it's my own personal secret agent test for insanity. But Joy's cigarette was fine, it was even better than fine, it had some lipstick on it. I was wondering what had happened to her with the Dalkon Shield and I had a feeling she wanted to tell me. So when she came back to the bar I asked her.

"If you don't mind telling me, what exactly happened to you?"

She leaned her elbows on the bar, took a breath, and told me her tale.

"Well, I was around eighteen, I'm thirty-four now, and it's so damn stupid, because I thought I was gay at the time. I even had a girl friend and wasn't even screwing around with men, but I had this IUD anyways. One night I started getting feverish, I thought I was getting sick so I laid down, but then I started going into convulsions and my parents had to rush me to the hospital, I was still living at home. . . . I didn't know what the hell was going on, but the pain was incredible, it was killing me. I passed out when I got to the hospital and didn't wake up for twenty-four hours. When I came to a nurse was in the room, I had all these tubes in my arms, I asked her if my appendix had been removed. She didn't answer. She just ran out of there and said, "The doctor better speak to you." So the doctor came in and I remember it was like he was towering over my bed, he didn't even sit down, I mean at least he could have done that, but instead he starts telling me like it was nothing, that my IUD had ruptured inside me, that I was lucky to be alive, but they had to remove all my female organs and I was now permanently sterile, and I would never have kids." She had spoken real fast but now took a long draw on her cigarette. "Those doctors gutted me like a fish."

I had trouble swallowing my beer. I was speechless, it's not every day you meet someone who tells you a story like that. I imagined some doctor sticking his hand inside her past the wrist and scraping with a spoon or knife till it was all smooth and empty inside, like a hollow red marble. I looked deeply into her eyes through the cigarette smoke and I liked her more than ever. For years I had been looking for a way to describe how I felt, and she had put it so perfectly, so simply: gutted like a fish. It had stopped raining and I was relieved, but I stayed till the bar closed and that night Joy and I became lovers.

SUMMER CAMP

When I was thirteen my parents sent me to summer camp. It was my present for having done so well in my Bar Mitzvah that past April. It was an all-sports camp in Pennsylvania and I went with a friend from Hebrew school. We lived in a large tent with four other boys and we were in the division for thirteen and fourteen year olds.

There were lots of playing fields and a large lake and I made the all-star teams in baseball and soccer, but the summer was a complete horror because I hadn't started puberty. There were fifty boys in my age group and I was the only one who didn't have pubic hair. They'd all run around the shower house nude and I'd stand there in my underwear and brush my teeth in the sink. I also missed out on the masturbation contests and the exchange of dirty magazines. Each night I would pray that I'd wake up and find hair. But it didn't happen that summer. I was forced to take showers at six A.M. or late at night and I changed my clothes when the other boys in the tent were asleep. I lived in fear of being seen. I was considered a good athlete, but I made no friends. The boy I came with drifted away from me.

Then halfway through the summer I got poison ivy. Dennis, the head counselor, had the jars of calamine lotion in his tent. He was the most popular counselor in our division and he walked around the shower house with a tremendous erection. He was considered the best-looking counselor by the girls' camp across the lake and he was our best softball player. He was tall and muscular with dark curly hair and a beautiful white smile. Dennis was probably twenty-five or so that summer. I went to him one night when the itching had become bad and the poison ivy had spread all over my body.

He said he'd help me put it on where I couldn't reach, but that we should go to the shower house where the light was better. We walked up there and went to the back near the toilet stalls. No one was in there and Dennis had me take my shirt and pants off. I stood there in my underwear and he kneeled in front of me. He opened the jar and began to spread the lotion on my stomach and legs. A queasy feeling came over me that has marked almost every erotic experience I've ever had. He said, "You have it there too, don't you?"

"I'm not sure," I said.

"Well, let's have a look," he said and he pulled

41

my underwear down. I was scared, I knew my penis was small.

"I'm not very big, I guess," I said.

"Don't worry," Dennis said, "you have plenty of time to grow."

He was the only person who saw me nude that summer and he was kind. He took some of the lotion and spread it lightly on my penis. Then we heard someone on the gravel outside and Dennis pulled my underwear up and rubbed some of the lotion on my shoulders. A kid came in and used one of the toilets. Dennis had me get dressed and he gave me the jar of calamine, so I'd have my own, and he walked me to my tent with his hand on the back of my neck.

I did feel a little funny about what happened that night and so I stayed away from Dennis, but I sort of hoped that he would pay more attention to me anyways and make me one of his favorites, but he didn't. Then towards the end of camp he was sitting watch one night by the fire. I was coming back from a movie with my tent mates and he called me over. When I got near him he whispered to me, "Has your voice changed yet?" And I knew what he meant, I knew what he was getting at, but I pretended I didn't, I said, "It cracked a few times when I sang during my Bar Mitzvah."

"That happens to everybody," he said, "but is your voice changing now?"

"No, not yet," I said and I felt embarrassed.

"That's O.K.," he said and we both looked at

42

the fire. Then he said, "You better get to bed, it's time to sleep."

Camp ended a few days later and I never went back. My friend from Hebrew school, though, continued to go there for several years. He was getting very good at basketball and after one summer I saw him in school and he told me that Dennis had been thrown out of camp. It was the big scandal of the summer. Dennis had been found in the showers sucking on two boys.

Ever since then I've often thought of how Dennis must have left the camp in shame. And I've thought about him out there somewhere in the world and I've wondered if I'll ever see him again. Sometimes I've let myself picture it in my mind. I figure we'll meet on some street or in a restaurant and he'll look the same and I'll go up to him and I'll say, "Dennis, my voice has changed."

*I WAS ON the subway late coming back from
The Four Seasons and a black man held on to the
pole in front of me and said to all the people, "I
have a story to tell you. Please listen to me. I fell
onto the tracks and was electrocuted and burned. And
the cops were the ones who pushed me and they said
I was running to get away from them and fell. They
lied and now half my face is missing. I have lost an
ear. I need money for surgery." He spoke well and
he was holding a dirty towel to his face and I could
see a skin graft covering his cheek, it was a square
patch of tight, light colored skin, and it was coming
apart at the edges and I could see blood. On the
same side of his head there was no ear, just stitches
and a hole. He collected money in a Mets hat and
went to the next car.*

*At the next stop a Latino family of three came
on and the mother was pregnant with another. The
father begged in Spanish, but they didn't get much
money, they didn't know that the other guy had been
in our car and he was a tough act to follow. I wanted
to explain to them why people weren't giving, but
they didn't speak English.*

*I got off the subway at the Spring Street station
and walked past the Hispanic groceries which are
open late at night. People were out sweating, moving, listening to merengue, and waiting to explode
and clutch one another, all of them sexy and cocky*

44

in their cheap clothes, and I wondered how to up the pace, how to make it more furious, and everywhere women were leaning on men leaning on cars, and then I got to Bowery Street and it was quieter. I felt lonely and I thought of Joy and I wished she would shave her legs. I walked towards Delancey and a bum was passed out, lying beside a building, and I saw that he had no arms and there was a can tied around his neck for money. I got to the corner and waited for the light to change and I thought to myself, men without hands can't really beg.

ETHAN

I wonder if I knew loneliness when I knew Ethan. He was my best friend for fourteen years. I still remember the first time I saw him, we were both three and we were the youngest of all the neighborhood kids and so we were put together one day when all the parents brought their children to Ethan's house. I remember that we were told to hold hands, to stick together, so we hid from the big kids, as we would always call them, under the brick grill in the back yard. That's how it began, but how it ended I don't really remember because there was no last time, like a first time, just a slow fade.

We grew up on the big lake behind our house and we learned to do everything together. We were inseparable every long summer and every weekend. (Ethan went to Catholic school during the week and so I didn't see him then, and the summer I went to camp was our only one apart). He was always much larger and heavier than me, and he was olive-skinned with brown hair—and I was pale and white with long red hair. And where he had strength, I had speed, so we were a good combination. We'd call each other every day and if I think hard I can still remember his phone number, 555-3454, and we'd always say, "Whatta you wanna do?" "I don't know whatta you wanna do?" We'd go back and forth like that and never figure anything out, but it didn't matter to me, I loved to be bored with Ethan.

Our domain was our lake and everything in our neighborhood had *the* before it as if there were only one big lake in the world, and only one island, *the* island, and only one field, *the* field. On the big lake we fished and rowed boats, and we did our swimming in the little lake, which the big lake fed into through the waterfall. On the beach of the little lake all the mothers would put their beach chairs in the same place every day to watch us and I remember the way they looked in their bathing suits. Ethan's mother always sat nervous in the shade and my mother swam a lot with her long hair piled on top of her head so it wouldn't get too wet. And when Ethan and I were young we dug holes all afternoon long on the edge of the shore and a hole was good when you hit the smooth clay at the bottom that felt slick in your hands. When we got older the goal was to swim to the dock and Ethan was the first between us to do that, but I was the first to dive.

We all loved the little lake yet no one swims there

anymore and for a couple of years my father was the only one who still went. He'd lie there and sleep in the late afternoon after driving all day. He's always slept wherever he's gone, so in a way he didn't notice too much that he was alone, but after a while he stopped going too. When I'm home now I walk down to the beach sometimes and I sit on the one bench that hasn't been broken and I look at the spot on the lake where the dock used to be. And when Ethan and I were in high school we'd come sit on this bench, we were waiting to get our driver's licenses, and Ethan's older brother told us that if we sat there long enough we'd see the woman on the other side of the little lake look at her breasts in the bathroom mirror. So when I go home I sit there and I still look, because even though I've done a lot of things I've never done that.

Alongside the beach, divided by a row of trees, is the field where Ethan and I played baseball and kickball. The second base rock is still there, but all the other bases have healed, they were dirt spots and the grass has grown back. When I'm down there at the field now I stand on second base and I wish I had people to play with. Sometimes I stand on the pitcher's mound and go through some motions, but I don't think anyone has seen me and I remember when Ethan and I played kickball his shoe would always come flying off and the silver plates he wore for arches would come flying out too. There was a time when they strapped his feet at night into metal boots. When I'd go over his house I'd put my feet in them too and you couldn't move, he had to sleep flat on his back each night.

If Ethan and I weren't down at the field or swimming in the little lake, then we were fishing on the big lake, and he was the one who could tie knots and put the worms on the hook so they wouldn't fall off. He'd do all the work for the both of us, but I was the one with the luck and I think he resented that. The last time I was home I took out the rowboat that Ethan and I had used, and I don't fish anymore, but from the water I can see Ethan's backyard. His family moved away seven years ago and I like to look at the back of his house, I once knew it as well as my own. I've thought sometimes of asking the new people to let me in and look, I'd like to see it again, but I'd want the old furniture to be in place. Outside the kitchen there is a patio and Ethan and I would eat our lunch there in the summer and play thousands of games of gin rummy. And farther down in Ethan's backyard is a bench and we'd sit there in the winter and put on our ice skates and clomp the few feet to the lake's edge and skate all day. And when we were really young my father would tie my dog Nicky to a sleigh and he'd pull us on the ice, and Ethan and I would hang on for our lives and scream.

I stared at the yard for a while and I let the boat drift slowly by, I moved the oars a little, I didn't want anyone to think I was spying, and the next house after Ethan's is the Quaid house and it's for sale again.

It was on the Quaid dock that I hooked Ethan on the chin with my fishing lure and I swore to him that I didn't mean to do it and I cut the line and we ran to his mother with the hook still in his face, with the blood coming out of his fingers where he held it, and he was crying and she screamed and rushed him to the doctor. I didn't go with him and I collected the poles, and I had known that he was behind me when I began to cast, I'd seen him out of the corner of my eye, and I should have stopped but I didn't, I felt myself letting it happen and I'll never know why. We both forgot about it in time and he forgave me and the scar wasn't bad, yet he must think of me sometimes when he shaves.

I looked past the Quaid dock to the Quaid house and they moved away even before Ethan's family, and ever since no one has stayed in that little yellow house for long. The Quaids were alcoholic and Ethan and I were told by our parents to stay away and they had a lot of wild children and the smell of old beatings must still be on the walls. No one has ever been happy in that house, and it makes sense to me, the neighborhood can't change too much.

I picked up the speed of my rowing and I went to the end of the big lake and pulled the boat on shore. I looked back over the water and the trees that bend over it, and I could see Ethan's backyard and farther down my own. I could see all the houses, I know all the names, and every summer all the people on the lake would get together for a giant picnic down at the field. Ethan and I loved the picnic, there were games and prizes for the kids, and we'd wait all summer for it to happen, and I still wait, and we haven't had one in ten years, but I keep expecting things to get back to normal and that we'll have a picnic, but it never comes. So I keep trying to figure out when things grew up, when things ended. I mean how come I still think that the Quaid house is the Quaid house? How come I still think Ethan is my best friend and I haven't seen him in seven years?

I got back in my boat and I returned to my house and I tied the boat up. I went inside and I was feeling nervous, I'd seen seen his backyard and I'd seen the Quaid dock, but I needed more of him, so I started searching for the boxes of pictures that my mother has saved, I hadn't seen them in years. I found them in the large desk in the living room and there were pictures of Ethan and me. It was good proof for me to get my hands on, and in a lot of ways that's what it's all about, just finding evidence that it did happen, like having the second-base rock to stand on. And I found some photos near the bottom of one box that brought a lot of things together. They were pictures of Ethan and me wearing my father's old hats and raggy clothes and our faces were smeared with dirt. I didn't understand why at first and then I remembered that we used to play a game called bums. We'd lie in the leaves for hours near the road above my house and get as dirty as we wanted and not do a thing. We thought it was a great life to be a bum and we even wore our outfits on Halloween. I looked at those bum pictures and Ethan's eyes were happy and it was amazing to see that I had loved bums my whole life, I had thought it was just a recent affection.

BEFORE AIDS, WHEN *herpes was big, I had a few venereal diseases. The gentleman shopper and I used to go to the VD clinic together. It was better than going alone. We'd sit on the plastic chairs and look at the pictures on the wall. They were blown-up color photographs of what happens to men and women, to their penises and vaginas, when they go untreated. The organs were pink and red and covered with scabs and lesions, swollen and destroyed, no longer recognizable. We usually went to the clinic nervous as hell a few weeks after one of our nights out (generally, we'd wait twenty-one days to give any infection a chance to show up) and nine times out of ten we didn't have any problem. We were lucky. And then we got even luckier when the whores started using condoms. Still, I got nicked a couple of times.*

Once I had a venereal wart and the doctor at the clinic sent me to a dermatologist. And the dermatologist wore goggles with magnifying lenses and a light in the middle, like a coal miner, to inspect me and he said he would have to anesthetize the area with a needle before burning the wart off with electricity. He put the needle in my penis and it seemed like the pain would never stop. I tried to think of Israeli soldiers, which is what I've done with pain since I was a kid, and just when I thought I was going to die he pulled the needle out. In a way it was beautiful. Another time I got a rash that isn't uncommon among street people and there were tiny lumps and I had to go back to the dermatologist and he used a liquid that was cold, yet somehow burned.

But I'm clean now. All my diseases are gone and I'm a lot more careful these days. I still do have some small scars, but you can't see them at night, in the dark, in my bed.

SHOW WORLD

It was so hot this one day in August that even when a little breeze stirred up it was like standing behind a bus running its motor. I went over to the Williamsburg Bridge thinking that it might be cool in its shade and cool near the water, but it was no good. I just stared at the East River's muscular currents and watched the water churn itself up brown with garbage and strain, and the steam there was worse than the street. I left the river and I walked back up Delancey and stopped at Ratner's, the only standing evidence of the once great Jewish occupation of this part of the Lower East Side. It was ten A.M. and I ordered *kasha varnishkes* and watched the old liver spotted couple across from me eat their cottage cheese blintzes. It was cool in there and if I'd had a paper I might have stayed awhile and eaten more of the free challah; but as it was I was out of the place by ten-forty-five and I was feeling pretty good because I had just flashed some Yiddish to the old lady at the register. It brought a big smile to her face when I said, *"Zei gazint,"* and I felt like a million bucks going out the door. But two yards up the block the heat and sun hit me in the face. It was my day off and I wanted desperately to go some place where I could sit in air-conditioning all day until the sun went down and the city cooled enough so that maybe then the air could be breathed and not eaten. I knew I could go to a theater, but I didn't want to pay the money, then it came to me—the Public Library on Fifth Avenue. I could read and look at girls and it wouldn't cost me a thing except what I had already paid in taxes. I took a subway and headed uptown.

I packed myself on the number 5 train with all the other people and I got off at Grand Central Terminal. The place was teeming with high-speed commuters and I went above ground and the sun was still glaring and I hate to be caught in too much sun because I squint and I worry about getting cancer on my eyelids. Thousands of office workers were pounding up Forty-second and everybody was soaking their shirts and blouses. I moved into the stream of people heading west, I was aiming for Fifth Avenue and the library, but the pace was slow and the street was jammed with buses and cars smoking, and the heat was driving me mad. I found myself cursing at everyone and everything, I even crossed my arms so it looked like I was holding myself, but really my fuck fingers were hidden in my armpits, and I'd wave my shoulders and declare a constant, silent fuck you to the whole street. The temperatures nowadays are unnatural and we've caused it and people were screaming and horns and sirens were screaming, and my fingers were digging holes into my skin, I thought I was going to boil, and I think I must have been blind for two blocks, because suddenly I was at the steps of the library. I ran up to the entrance and spun through the revolving doors into the lobby where the air-conditioning kissed me all over and said hello.

I slid my feet along the cool, shiny marble floor like ice skating and I went up the two flights of wide stairs to the wood-carved, high-ceilinged McGraw Rotunda. You couldn't hear New York outside and I bent my neck back and looked at the painting of heaven on the ceiling. Then I made a left into the reading room and it was almost cold in there and I passed down the long center aisle of the many tables, the room is half a football field in length, and I collapsed in a hard wooden chair and let my head sink to the desk. After a while I raised up again and my brain wasn't beating too bad anymore and I thought maybe I'd go ask for a book, a good mystery, when this tall Norwegianesque blonde walked by and it looked like she had ten pound weights in her breasts and they stuck straight out and I just sort of corkscrewed in my chair like someone had hit me in the cheek with a bag of quarters. All the other perverts were watching her too, the reading room is filled with them, homos and heteros, and I felt my whole-life-want circulate somewhere near the tops of my thighs and I felt sick and nauseous.

She was wearing a halter top, with a white bra that showed itself in one delicate, misplaced strap on her round, smooth shoulder. She was wearing a pair of shorts that went to her mid-thigh and she was about six foot and all of her was fine muscle and a dancer's posture to support those beautiful breasts. She wore no makeup and was pure with one honey-colored braid going down to the middle of her back. She sat down for just an instant and then went back up to the front desk and was directed to the card-catalog room to the right and when I couldn't see her anymore I wanted to run to her table and throw my face into her chair and rub it in the wood. But I steadied myself and she came back and sat down to work in earnest for a while.

She sneezed once and I envied the young man sitting across from her who said, God bless you. She thanked him and then a few minutes after that she lifted up one of her knees and pressed it to her chest and leaned over her books. A bit of ivory cleavage was revealed to me and also a slight shadow that ran along the inside of her thigh into her shorts. She absentmindedly twirled a pencil and I couldn't stop staring. She was a mirage in human form of everything above and beyond sex that had ever been denied me. Rather than give me a hard-on, she drained me and starved me, I wasn't sure if I was going to collapse to the floor or make a mad rush at her and commit some crime that I'd have no control over.

The whole day was welling up inside me, I couldn't be outside in the heat, but I couldn't be where I'd see this girl, in fact I felt like I couldn't be around her another thirty seconds. I could have gone to the periodical room, but I didn't even want to be in the same building. I rose out of my seat and I half ran out of there, I wondered if she noticed, but I didn't look, and I went through the silent, cool marble halls and down the white steps until I spun outside once more and stood between the Greek columns above Fifth Avenue in the hot bath that was the midday hour.

There was only one air-conditioned place for me to go and I started running and if I hadn't been sweating, I might have been crying. I felt it pulling me and I ran the three crosstown blocks and paid my dollar, got four tokens, and went into Show World.

"Come on fellas, hot juicy pussy, good lickin' suckin' and fuckin,' beautiful girls with beautiful pussies, girls on girls, girls on boys, juicy, juicy vaginas, one flight up, one flight down, live sex, let's move along, dicks in cunts, and tits and pussee, pussseee, pussseee!"

I was in the front room with the rest of the men, it was busy since it was the lunch hour, and the air-conditioning was working and the colored light bulbs were flashing, and I went past the wall that held the dildos, double ended dildos, fake vaginas, vibrators, hydraulic penis extenders, strap-on rubber chests, leashes, girdles, leather masks, diapers, and rubber dolls, over to the glossy picture magazines where everybody usually warms up. I scanned the titles, Black Cunt, Shaved Cunt, Animal Sex, Bi-Girls, Blonde Girls, Asian Lust, Anal Passion, Female Domination, Big Babies, and picked out one called Super Big Titties. I strummed through the pictures, but all the breasts were terrible, flabby and spreading, and I put it back, then grabbed one called TV Action. There were pictures of pre-op transsexuals who still had their penises and could screw real women and wear bras gracefully at the same time. I put that back and accidentally touched the arm of the man next to me. He was wearing a dark cheap suit and his tie was undone and he said to me, "Eighteen years in the peep shows jerking off in front of women." Then the man with the loudspeaker shouted at all of us, "Buy the magazines, fellas, don't read 'em, move along, this isn't a library." And so I shuffled off to the rows of movie stalls and didn't say anything to the guy. I've been in and out of peep shows for a couple of years and that's the first time anyone has spoken to me. No one every makes eye contact or talks unless they're trying to cruise, and that guy wasn't cruising.

I shook it off and went along the movie stalls looking for something I'd like. I went down one hall and it was semi-dark and I made sure no one was following me and the movies are listed on the doors with a little picture and description and I chose one called *Women in Prison*. I went in the stall, it's about the size of a confessional or a closet, and I braced myself against the door because there was no lock. I slipped in two tokens and the movie started up, and I got my penis out. Show World is an up-to-date peep show and the movie showed on a little TV screen planted in the wall and the action picked up where the last guy's token had run out. A busty woman prison guard was putting her nightstick through the bars of a cell and a nude blonde was sucking on it. I was stroking myself and I noticed out of the corner of my eye that a hand had poked through the little hole in the wall near my left leg and was making grabbing motions. I stuffed my penis back in my pants and got out of there before my two tokens had even run out, it might have been the guy in the suit after all.

I went to the second floor where for a two-dollar token you can talk to a woman over a phone and look at her in a glass booth. Usually I jerk off in one of the movie stalls or in one of the live sex stalls where you watch through a glass window, but I felt like doing something different. The women stood in front of their booths wearing lingerie and plenty of men stalked about. Every type of guy off the street, from businessmen to tourists from the Port Authority, comes to the peep shows to try to relax. I exchanged my two tokens and another three-fifty and got two silver tokens and chose an older black women who was smiling and laughing and who looked like she had large breasts under her kimono. I told her I wanted her and she took me to my side of the booth and gave me a paper towel, which I thought was nice. I closed the door behind me, got my pants down, put one of the tokens in and picked up the phone. The screen started to rise and light dimmed on my side and she was on the other side of the large glass window and the kimono was off and I was upset. Somehow that flimsy garment had hidden her very large belly and the breasts were huge like I thought, but the nipples were barely discernible brown stains. I was disappointed, but my penis was hard and I wanted to come. She spoke in her phone and I listened in mine.

"Baby just put some money in the envelope I'm slipping in and we can have a real good time." A dirty envelope came through a crack in the side of the glass and I put in a dollar and shoved it back. She put it in her purse and then got on a stool and lifted her legs and spread them and rested her heels against her side of the glass. I tried to get a look at her, and I could see some black hair and some of her lips, but she was sitting on most of her vagina. She talked to me over the phone.

"Come on baby play with your big dick, wouldn't you like to stick your dick between my titties? Fuck my titties."

I held the phone with my left hand and rubbed

myself with my right hand and she was pushing her tits together. She smiled at me and said, "Feel good?"

I felt obliged to talk so I said, "Yes," and then I added and I don't know why, "You're very pretty."

"Thank you," she said and then, "come on baby pull on your dick and put it in my wet cunt."

I was just about to come, but then the screen started going down and she told me to put another token in. The light came back on and I dug the coin out of my pocket and put it in the slot, but the screen didn't rise up. I tried to tell her over the phone, but it was dead. I knocked on the glass and I shouted, "It's broken." Then there was a knock at my door and I pulled up my pants and she was there with a man and he came into my stall and banged the coin box with his fist and the screen started to rise. She scurried over to her side, the light went off, he took his time getting out of there, and I closed the door. I got my pants undone and picked up the phone and she was nude again on the other side.

"Just pull on that dick and come all over, I want to see you come."

I had already lost valuable time and I got myself erect again and I stared at what I could see of her vagina and she urged me to come before my money ran out. I closed my eyes and thought of the girl in the library and then I came and the whore cheered me over the phone and the screen started to come down. The light came on and I had made four drops on the black floor. I squeezed the tip to get a little more out, then I wiped my cock and my hands with the paper towel. And sometimes I feel sorry for my penis, I make it do things it probably doesn't want to do, but it obliges anyways, and must think that everything is for a higher purpose.

I got my pants up and got out of the stall and the guy who had fixed the coin box went in with a mop since my lady in the kimono had another customer already waiting. I said goodbye to her and I went down the stairs and out the front room past the magazines and rubber organs and emerged back on to Forty-second into the throngs of people in a way that no one would notice where I came from. The heat was still terrible, but I didn't fight it. I thought that maybe I'd go back to the library. I figured I could sit right next to the girl now and it wouldn't even bother me. So I headed for Fifth Avenue and I thought I'd get a good book, but I made a stop along the way. The marquis read LIVE GIRLS!! INCREDIBLE SEXUAL ACTS 25¢, and I went in.

I WANTED TO
KNOW WHY

I've been thinking about suicide ever since Roy Laudner killed himself. He was a handsome boy whom everyone knew and said good things about. He was president of the ecology club. And what stood out about him to me was that the handlebars on his bike were the old-fashioned type, and I didn't know why he didn't have the ten-speed handlebars like everyone else. His bike even had mud guards and an old, fat leather seat. He had curly brown hair which my sister wrote about in the poem. She said it was like a "wreath of olive leaves wrapped around your head." Her poem about Roy is still one of the most beautiful things I've ever read, it was written like a letter to him. I remember the last time I saw him he stopped with that black bike of his at my friend Ethan's driveway. We had been playing basketball. And it was a cool fall day and we talked a little while, Roy knew me because of my sister, and I pretended

I didn't notice his old-fashioned handlebars. I was pretty happy after he rode away thinking what a nice guy. And I felt cool in front of my best friend Ethan that a guy in high school would talk to me. I also remember he had a catch with me down at the rec field and didn't make me feel like a little kid. He was kind to me and I never really knew why.

And then it spread all over town that he hanged himself. My sister ran around our house screaming and crying, I stayed out of her way, and she ran into her room and slammed the door, shrieking. I wasn't sure who it was at first, and then I realized it was the guy with the bike. Slowly the facts started coming out and we all found out that he had hanged himself nude in the basement and was found by his sister. Supposedly she touched him once or twice and said, "Roy, quit fooling around," and then realized he was dead and ran out of the house. What struck me was thinking about him hanging there nude. I always have thought that must've been the first shock, seeing her brother all nude. I bet she even laughed, she was only fourteen, and I bet she's got some secret shame about seeing her brother's penis and feeling excited with him being dead. Over the years I would ask my sister to tell me all she knew about the suicide, I wanted to know every detail.

When my sister wrote the poem it was about how Roy might've loved her and she had loved someone else, but now that he was dead she knew she loved him, only it was too late to say, "I love you." So she felt, like everybody did in their own way, that it was her fault, but it wasn't. The rumor was that he wanted to go to college, but his parents couldn't afford it. And that seemed to explain why he had the old-fashioned handlebars. So one day Roy stayed home sick from school.

I tried to imagine him walking around his house naked, carrying that rope. What was he thinking, was he crying, when he threw it over the beam and went swinging down, oh Roy, why? I asked my sister if he left a note and she didn't think he did. My parents said things like, "See? Parents should never hesitate to give to their children." Somehow when things like that happen my parents start feeling all high and mighty because my sister and I haven't killed ourselves. I hate it when they act like that.

At the end of the school year the yearbook came out. And we all skimmed through it looking for pictures of Roy. And sure enough, there he was sitting in the stands of a football game and it seemed to me his face stood out above all the rest. He was in a large crowd and everyone was shouting and smiling, except for Roy who looked so quiet and erect. And I thought, was he thinking about killing himself at that very moment? There was another one of him in the stands and it had the same eerie feeling, you knew he was dead now. The yearbook was dedicated to him, he was the only one who had died, and it was at this time that I began to fantasize about my own suicide. Usually at night I'd put myself to sleep wondering if (and hoping) the whole town would cry for me the way they did for him. I even experimented in front of the mirror with a towel around my neck, but I didn't know how to tie it right (my father has always told me I'm no good with my hands), and I have never learned. I had only talked to Roy Laudner twice in my life, but I started mourning for him. My mother and sister didn't know it, but I'd take out the yearbook and look at him in those stands so alone, and I'd look at his senior picture in his tie, and I'd read my sister's beautiful poem, and I'd cry for him. It was my secret that I missed him.

In eighth grade a few years after it happened, my teacher started talking about suicide and she brought up Roy. She said, "You never know why someone might kill himself, but most likely it is when he has a problem that he can't talk about. When Roy Laudner killed himself a few years ago," and then my ears pricked up, she was talking about my Roy Laudner, how dare she say his name out loud, I was hating her, "they found in his dresser drawer that he had tied all his socks in knots." I wanted to scream, how did you know that? how can you tell everyone Roy's secrets? By this time I had thought so much about Roy Laudner's suicide, had played it over so many times in my head, that I almost felt I had walked down his basement stairs with him, looked at his naked body, watched him tie the rope (he was an Eagle Scout), and stared at him swaying and swinging, just like his sister. I just didn't want to think of Roy tying his socks in knots and the teacher had spoken about him as if he were nobody, and like everybody she blamed the parents for not seeing their son's problem.

The following year my sister started going out with Roy's younger brother, Paul, who looked just like Roy, the same tight curly hair, handsome face, and that smile that made you feel like you were friends. And so one day I went over to the Laudner house with my sister and I met the whole family. Roy's sister, the one who found him, was pretty and I had a lot of questions I wanted to ask her, but I couldn't. And you could see Roy in her face and I liked her, but she was older than me. I guess I liked her the same way my sister liked Paul. The two girls went to talk and Paul took me to the basement down the old dirty wooden stairs to show me a model he was working on. And I tried to look at the rafters without him noticing and figure out which one, and how did Roy do it (with a ladder maybe?), and then I saw his black bike old and lost in the corner with tools and broken furniture. I remembered Roy riding it, his arms bent to the handles, and then I wondered who had cut him down, who had held his dead naked body? And my mind would not stop and I never wanted to leave there, I wanted to figure it all out. I felt somehow that if I stayed there forever, I could watch it all happen again and I would know. But then Mrs. Laudner called us upstairs for dinner and I looked back at the basement to remember exactly how it was and to imagine Roy hanging above all the clutter.

When everyone was at the table I looked at the parents trying to see their pain and loss which I thought must be so evident (my parents had said they would not go on living if it was them), but I could see nothing in their faces. Yet I knew it was there surrounding all of us. I excused myself to go to the bathroom, but instead went to Roy's room which was also down the hall. My sister had pointed it out earlier and had whispered that it had been left untouched since he died. The door was open a crack and I went in. The whole room was neat and the bed was perfectly made. I saw a pair of sneakers by the closet and his jeans hanging over his desk chair. And a science book was open, he must have been studying before he died. I wished that I would find a note that no one else had seen and then I would know why, but it wasn't there of course, and I stepped out growing too scared to continue and made sure to shut the door the same amount it had been open. I went to the bathroom to flush the toilet and returned to the dining room. I was thirsty from my adventure and I asked Paul, "Roy, could you pass the milk?" Everyone stopped talking, I had evoked his name. I stared down at my plate unable to move and I was saying to myself over and over again so that God would hear, "I'm sorry, I'm sorry," and I wished that I were dead.

A COUPLE OF years ago one night I was drunk on the lower West Side and weaving my way along the waterfront piers. I saw a man leaning against a fence and I stopped sixty yards from him and turned my head in his direction. I waited, then turned my head again, I had never done it before, but I knew somehow to communicate to him in code. I'm a natural at these things. I didn't look back again, but listened to his steps as he came alongside me. He was an old man, in his sixties, and he was short with thin, dry gray hair along the top of a very round, sun-marked head. He was dressed comfortably in leisure slacks and a windbreaker. He had an accent and it turned out he was Italian and a major chef at a big restaurant. After some small talk about New York dining, he asked, "Do you want to love me tonight?" I didn't like the question and didn't want to answer, so I mumbled something and let him think it meant whatever he wanted it to mean. He took my arm and led me through the fence and down a small concrete slope until we were beneath the giant wooden dock. We were just a few feet from the water and he asked me very politely, he had fine manners, if I wanted to screw him or if I wanted a blow job. I said blow job and I leaned against one of the beams and he went down carefully on his knees, he was old. It smelled of salt and garbage down there and he undid my pants. He took me in his mouth and he was an expert and it felt so good that I actually touched his gray old head. I tried to pretend it was one of the million pretty girls I saw on the street and that worked pretty good and I lurched and came in his mouth and he ate all of it, and all the while he made little whimpering happy sounds that men make (not women) when they have a cock in their mouth. I zipped up my pants and he was still kneeling and it was dark, but I could see how his round face glowed. I had a violent flash for an instant, which happens to me sometimes, and I saw how easily I could kick in his head and shove him in the water. But I let it pass through me like a breeze and when I was clear I gave him a hand so he could stand. I started to walk away and he asked me if I'd be back tomorrow night, and I said, I don't know.

BOOZE RUN

I was walking home late one night from Joy's around three in the morning and I saw a bum do his best to run into Spring Street park. He collapsed on a bench and his head was in his hands.

"Whatsa matter?" I asked.

"I got jackrolled by some junkies . . . I'm all shook up."

"What did they do?"

"I just got my last twenty cents and so I got a bottle. And then they came up from behind and took the bottle and when I didn't have any money they threw me down, goddamn junkies."

Three other bums showed up and one of them was old J. B. Britten. He was the oldest and kindest and held court there in Spring Street park to comfort the bum who got beaten by the junkies. J.B. has no teeth in his long, lined American face and he has these clear blue eyes, which is surprising for an alcoholic bum, it's the last part of him holding on and not yet dead. His long legs were crossed like a gentleman and he was soothing the others like an officer in a bunker, "We'll get another bottle. Let's not worry, Rocky's will be open." But they were afraid of the junkies, afraid to go on a booze run and get beat up. Indiana, one of J.B.'s friends said, "Goddamn nigger junkies wreck everything, no one leaves us bums in peace." So feeling brave and unafraid of the streets I offered to go on a booze run for them. They pooled their money, nickels and dimes from begging, and J.B. delegated Billy to act as my guide to find Rocky's. Billy was the youngest bum and fresh out of detox that day so he was in pretty good shape for such a mission. Every four weeks or so in a bum's life he gets scraped off the street and put in a city detox center. They shower him off (hose you down, the bums call it) and give him food and bed for about five days. He gets new used clothes and then badly needing a drink he's sent back out on the street. Within two days he's covered again with bugs and grime and blood. J.B. explained it to me, "There's a difference between wanting and needing a drink."

So Billy and I went off to Rocky's. He told me he was a vet, and though most of the bums in the Bowery are WWII or Korean War vets, I assumed he meant Vietnam, I asked him what it was like.

"I was eighteen, man, and we got off the chopper right in the fucking jungle, right in the fucking action, I started running I was scared shit bullets were flying it was a fucking ambush and I was running, and all of a sudden I feel something real hot on my back, and I think o my god jesus christ I'm hit, and I reach my hand back and it's the brain matter of my *paesan*, his head was blown off and I was covered with my *paesan*'s brains man. I keep running and when we stop I go into convulsions, suddenly I have epilepsy and the medic gives me a joint of opium and said it would make me feel better."

We walked past my building, and then past the whores on the corner. Goldie was there and she smiled at me, remembered me, and she and the others said, "Goin' out?" And I said, "Not tonight," and Billy kept on telling his story.

"I was hooked on opium and hash you know in Nam, came back to the States and became a junkie shootin' up all the time. That's what this country did for me, right, but I couldn't get the money up to be a junkie no more, so I'm nothin' but an alcoholic bum, and tomorrow I'm supposed to go to the VA for my epilepsy, I'm all fucked up."

We stopped in front of an old, black from soot, brick building and Billy scratched at a rusted metal plate in the wall, this was Rocky's. The plate slid back and there was a screen with a square cut out of it, big enough for a hand, and Billy said, "Rocky, it's me Billy, I want a bottle." An upturned palm came out of the hole, I tried to look in but it was too dark. Billy dumped the collected change in Rocky's palm. I looked out for junkies and could hear the coins being counted. Billy was getting nervous, "It's all there Rocky, we counted." The hand came back out with a bottle of Thunderbird wine and Billy grabbed it quick and shoved it in his pants. The metal plate slid back in place.

We walked back fast and all the old bums' faces lit up when we got there. J.B. said, "I knew they'd come back." Billy being the youngest wanted to assert his trustworthiness in the group and said, "I told you I'd come back, I wouldn't keep that bottle for myself." They let the bum who got jackrolled have the first hit. He stopped shaking and complaining and the bottle was passed down the bench. When J.B. took a long hard swig he started hacking bad, but with dignity managed to spit just a little. All the bums are rotted out inside, there's nothing to throw up but their own guts, and their bodies just gag out of reflex—the dry heaves. They offered me a shot, but I refused. J.B. was glad. "Don't let the big A kill you," he said. The bottle was empty too quickly for the bums and it was a long time before the people would be out that they could panhandle a few coins from. I said goodbye and left them chattering and complaining, like people everywhere that's what they do best.

MY GREAT-AUNT DOLL

My great-aunt Doll calls me from Queens once a month to see how I'm doing. She tells me to eat alphabet soup because the letters will be good for my brain. She says, "Eat Camp-Bells," and she asks me when I'm going to visit because she wants to take me to NBO and buy me a suit. I do visit two or three times a year, but after lunch, usually scrambled eggs, lox, bagels, herring, and onions, I pass out on her little couch at which time she inspects my scalp to see if I'm balding. She used to be a manicurist in some of the big hotels and so she knows a lot about hair. The last time I was there she told me that I burned my scalp in the sun, and I told her I never go in the sun. Somehow I always manage to put off going to NBO until my next visit, usually I bribe her with a game of Scrabble.

She's in her seventies and she lives off her savings in that crowded one room apartment and her life changed terribly when she had one of her very large breasts removed. She used to be a very sexy lady, and she was married several times and she had lots of gentlemen friends who left their slippers under her bed even as she got older. But with the breast gone she's lost her confidence and she says, "No man wants half a woman." She's very open with me and when I requested, she showed me the scar where her breast used to be. It was thin and red and there was no more nipple.

She called the other day and told me that she went to a specialist to see about an implant, but he told her that she's too old, that her skin is too thin. She said to me, "It's no good to be alone." And she was disappointed at the doctor's news, but he was kind to her. She said he was young and good looking and was nice enough to button her shirt when the visit was over.

I PICKED UP Joy at the bar where she works and we went back to her place. She took some of the black plastic bags off the sculptures she was working on and I looked at the damp clay. She was having a model sit for her and rather than sculpt the woman's whole figure, there were just pieces of her body: a shoulder, a calf, an arm, and a stomach leading into a groin. We stared at them for a minute or two, then Joy sprayed the pieces with water and covered them back up.

We got undressed and climbed into bed. Her body was cool next to mine and I held her, then sucked on her breasts. She has large brown nipples, most of her breast is nipple, and when I had them in my mouth she pressed her hand against the back of my head in an urgent way, and I was very happy. Later, when I was inside her, my eyes were closed and I thought of other women. I thought of this teacher in high school who I had always desired, and I thought of the groin in the plastic bag on the other side of the room, and I thought of the Hispanic girl in the grocery who had been giving me the eye. After I came I rolled off Joy and fell into that deep sleep that comes sometimes after sex.

When I awoke, Joy was asleep and I looked at the curve of her back and at the nubs of her spine that showed. I thought of all the people I'd slept with in my life, all the bodies I'd touched, and how they would fill the whole room. In my mind I saw all of them nude with their hairy mounds and hanging breasts, their bodies white and lifeless, lining the walls of Joy's apartment, pressing against one another, hovering around me. I wanted to go back to sleep to put them out of my mind, but I couldn't, so I woke Joy up and asked her to talk to me for just a little while, and she did. When I let myself look around the room again, it was empty, except for the shapes under the plastic bags.

MY NEW
RED HAT

Hanging above my father's desk on its original blue string is my little graduation card from nursery school. On the front of the card is my name in capital letters and a glued-on watercolor picture of a policeman. On the back in my teacher Miss Carol's neat printing is an inscription about me. It goes like this:

> Alexander, says that he wants to be a policeman: " 'Cause I like their hats!" We think Alexander will be a teacher. He is a good listener and when he says something he really means it. Alexander also loved to sing and tell stories for his his friends at Lenape.

The card ends there and every time I read it I wish she had written more.

The incredible thing is that I'm still a hat lover. And that helps to explain why I was so hurt when my doorman's cap was stolen. It was the first day of the fall season and the menus and napkins were being changed and so was my outfit. I was given my new red hat and jacket by the Four Seasons' in-house seamstress and the new color felt great. After the long summer wearing pink I couldn't stop admiring how good I looked in red.

I was on the job about a half hour in my new outfit, swinging my whistle the way a lifeguard does, when this older well-dressed woman went walking by me heading in the direction of Park Avenue. For some intuitive street reason I kept my eyes on her and when she was just past my canopy a black man jumped out from behind a van, he must have been crouching there, and in one quick yank he had her purse. She screamed, he ran, and without even thinking I was after him. He went up the side steps that lead to the Seagram's plaza and I was only ten feet behind him. The plaza wasn't too crowded and I was sprinting all out and my hat blew off and I didn't bother to pick it up. He turned around for an instant and saw me, then cut across the busy sidewalk into the traffic on Park Avenue. I followed him and I almost got hit by a taxi, but was able to catch up to him at the concrete island in the middle of the street. He had to stop there when a truck on the other side was coming down too fast. I yelled, "Purse snatcher!" and dug my fingers into the back of his jacket. He spun around and with his free hand in a fist he slapped me hard across the face. It was like a small gun going off and I was blinded and when I could see again he was aiming to kick me and somehow I moved in time and it glanced off my hip, but it was enough to bring me down. I think I kneeled on purpose. He ran across the street and one man made a grab for him, but missed, and from my knees I watched the purse snatcher run until he turned left on Fifty-fourth Street and disappeared.

I stood up slow and retreated back across the avenue to the plaza. I went to get my hat and it was gone. I panicked. I ran to my right and then to my left. I felt like a little boy, I wanted to cry. I ran to the wall above the fountain and I climbed up there and looked everywhere, but I saw no one with my red hat. Then I had the idea that it might have been returned to the canopy. I sprinted back down the side steps and when I got to the restaurant's doors the only person there was the woman whose bag was stolen.

I told her I didn't get him and she was a tough, old rich lady and rather than cry she kept on saying, "Goddamnit." I didn't tell her about my hat, but I was worried as hell that one of the owners would see me. Everything has got to be perfect at The Four Seasons and my one hope was that the seamstress had put Dimitri's new red hat in his cubbyhole in the coat room. But first I had to get the woman off my hands. I brought her into the lobby and gave her two quarters so she could call the police and her husband. Once she was in the phone booth I ducked

83

into the coat room and I walked to the back. I shut my eyes for a second and when I let myself look, Dimitri's red hat was there. I grabbed it and put it on.

I got out of the coat room and went into the customers' bathroom which I'm not supposed to do. But I winked at the Haitian attendant and locked myself into one of the marble stalls. I took the hat off and put it on the hook on the inside of the door. I lowered the cover on the toilet and I sat down. I leaned my face against the smooth green and black wall and the coolness of the marble soothed me where I had been slapped. It was the first time I had ever been hit in the face and I took some consolation in that fact. I didn't stay in there too long and I was able to slip out without any customers seeing me.

I went back to work and I didn't see the woman again. She must have used the phone quickly and left while I was in the bathroom. I half hoped that she would show up with her husband and give me a five or something, but she never did. And I worked hard that night as if nothing had happened, but I did feel this need to punish myself. All night long I dug my thumbnails into the sides of my hands and I curled my toes in my shoes when I ran to the avenue. It helped me not to think about things. It helped me not to think about somebody out there wearing my red hat and looking at himself in the mirror.

NICKY

I dreamt of my old dog Nicky. I dreamt that I
was telling him that I would be right back to play
with him and he waited in our yard, behind the fence.
And in my dream I was so happy to see him, but
somehow I didn't make it back to the yard and I
woke up. I hadn't thought about Nicky for years.

He was given to me when I was three and he
died when I was seventeen. He died a few months
before my Grandfather. When I was a kid Nicky slept
every night in my room and if I get down on my
hands and knees the carpet still smells. He was a
good-looking dog, large and black, and because he
was part husky, he had blue eyes. He always wanted
to run and so I'd take him to the woods without a
leash and I'd pack food for the both of us. He loved
me and I thought I was a real dog owner because I
used to let him kiss me on the lips. Once in a while
he liked to get loose, he was ingenious at finding holes

in our fence, and he'd be gone for a day or two, but he always came home. It occurs to me now that he probably has children, but even if I found them I wouldn't get Nicky back.

When he was fourteen things started going bad. He went blind, his back legs went stiff, he smelled of dying dog, and he had fatty tumors under his skin, so I didn't like to touch him anymore. One day he fell down the basement stairs and at the bottom he was on his side and he couldn't get on his feet, his paws were waving, twitching. His body rocked back and forth. A friend of mine was with me and we looked down those stairs. My friend had sort of a smile on his face and I didn't know what to do. I didn't want to touch Nicky. So I laughed and my friend laughed too.

A few weeks later my parents decided that Nicky was in too much pain and that he should be put to sleep. My father had to work the day of the appointment, so my mother and I took Nicky to the animal hospital. A vet examined him and agreed that Nicky was suffering too much. My mother went out to the waiting room and I stayed with the vet. He prepared a needle and told me that my job was to hold Nicky down. Then he said, "You're doing the best thing for the dog," and I looked at Nicky and he was peaceful and I thought that this must be the right time. But when the needle went in he started fighting and squirming, there was still life in him, he wasn't ready, and I wanted to say stop, but it was too late, the clear poison was draining and a tube was filling with Nicky's blood. I held him down and he fought, and maybe a milky gray eye rolled up at me, the last thing he saw, and I pushed my fingers into him, stay down Nicky, stop Nicky, and he was dead. My hands were still in his fur and the vet withdrew the needle and placed it gently on a table. I went out to the car and banged my hands on the steering wheel.

TRICK OR TREAT

Joy came over and when she kissed me I told her to leave. She had put her tongue in my mouth and the taste was terrible. She must have smoked a cigarette as she walked over and I had told her in the past never to smoke before she saw me and so I yelled at her, "Get the hell out of here. I can't stand the taste of cigarettes." I pushed her out of my room and slammed the door shut.

I looked at her through the peephole and she was standing there and her face was all distorted, her forehead was humongous and her chin was almost non-existent. She started crying which made it worse and she must have realized I was watching, because all of a sudden she shot out a grossly enlarged fuck finger right up to her side of the peephole. I reflexively jerked my head back in shock and when I ventured to look again she was running down the rickety, dirty stairs. But I knew she'd come back in a few days, it's a vicious cycle, and I wondered to myself, "Why does she want me? Can't she see what I am?"

When I turned away from the door I spotted the *Daily News* on the floor and there was a big ad that said, HALLOWEEN IS COMING! And whenever I think of Halloween I get this image in my mind of a woman in a kitchen. She's middle-class heavy in a house dress and apron, has large glasses, wears her light brown hair conservatively on her head and her kitchen is white and spotless. (I must have formed this picture from a very early school film on careers that said: "This is a housewife.") And in my vision she's at the sink and she's putting razors in apples, but because her back is to me I can't see how. She has a whole bowlful ready to go when the doorbell rings. She wipes her hands on her apron and goes to the door. A chorus of ghoulish, smiling kids sings, "Trick or treat, trick or treat," and she smiles back as she hands each one of them an apple. They are bathed in the yellow light of her porch, it's only six-thirty but dark because it's October, and she watches them run happily across her lawn and then shuts the door.

When I went around as a kid I was always eyeing each lady trying to figure out which one would put razors in apples. Every year we were warned by our parents and teachers not to eat anything until we came home and had it inspected. We were warned that many children died each year. But in my neighborhood we never got apples, though every Halloween

I hoped for one. I wanted to be the one who got the apple with the razor and beat the person at their own game: I found the razor! So after thinking about this for one second I realized why Joy and the others have wanted me, I'm an apple with a razor inside.

YOU CONNED US

My parents raised me to believe that as a Jew I was subject to termination at any time, so I should always try to keep a low profile. To this day they still get nervous when a Jew does something bad and it hits the newspapers. They figure it's the end for all of us, that one loud Jew will cause the rest of us to be gassed. Above my father's desk in his little office is the headline of an article that reads: NEW JERSEY LEADS THE NATION IN ANTISEMITIC ATTACKS. Next to it hangs a gun, so he's armed and ready, but when he retires he wants to go to Florida because he says, "In Florida it's too hot, but at least a Jew can be as loud as he wants."

But I wasn't raised only to fear death by resurgent Nazis. Rather, I was led to believe that my life was in critical condition all the time. I was constantly warned about infection and disease and accident. If I took a shower I couldn't go out with a wet head. If someone in school took a bite out of my sandwich I felt compelled to secretly throw it away. And it wasn't until I was seventeen that I realized that people drove their cars in the rain, all I had ever heard was, The roads are slippery, you'll die!

So I grew up in a state of constant preparation for disaster. My father had flashlights in every room and numerous small bank accounts and very little of anything was ever thrown away, everything was stored and kept just in case. It's an inherited anxiety and Jews of my family's background exist in the painful flux between miserdom and martyrdom. In miserdom they count and save everything they have, so that when they get to martyrdom they will know what they have lost.

When I was old enough my move to New York was to be my great escape from all this fear. But just before I was leaving New Jersey I got a phone call from my great-aunt Doll who when I was younger used to counsel me on ways I could lose a finger or an eye. And so she saddled me with some advice about New York that I'd like to forget, but it stays in my mind anyways and I walk around the city feeling like I did when I was a kid—with a subdued sense that catastrophe will strike at any moment. She said: "When you're on the sidewalk don't go too close to the edge because some maniac, and New York is filled with *meshuggas* so watch yourself, might push you in front of a bus. And don't walk in the middle be-cause I read in the *Post* that with all the construction things are falling off buildings left and right and in the middle is the most dangerous place to be. So just walk very close to the buildings, probably no more than an arm's length is safe.

"And the same thing with the subway, always have a token ready and STAND AGAINST THE WALL! A Hasidic boy was pushed in front of a train last week by a *shvartzer*. Be careful!"

I don't want to , but I constantly look at the tops of buildings and I hug the walls down in the subway. The general rule for self preservation that was taught to me is this: Expect the worst and maybe it won't happen to you. The worst that could happen to me according to my parents would be if I died prematurely. If that occurred I would bring them unimaginable amounts of *tsuris* and grief. And I was raised to bring my parents the opposite of *tsuris* which is *naches*. At the end of every Bar Mitzvah, including my own, the rabbi would say, "May your children continue to bring you *naches*." And that benediction was a prison sentence because *naches* not only meant happiness, it meant perfect grades and awards, acceptance to a fine school and a professional degree, and ultimately a Jewish marriage and healthy grandchildren. My sister has done beautifully, she's not married yet, but she's a doctor; I, on the other hand, began to bring my parents *tsuris* when I was eighteen and told them I wouldn't go to college. This hit them hard, especially my mother. And for once it was she who screamed and it must have come from somewhere deep in her liver, some old stored hatred, it was ugly, even her face, she yelled, "YOU CONNED US, GODDAMNIT. YOU CONNED US!" She saw my tears and I ran out of the house. She called after me and she said, "I'm sorry!" But I never told her that I heard that.

So I never went to college and they didn't stop loving me. Sometimes my father will say, "My son, the doorman." And that's good, they don't expect too much from me anymore, yet there are times when I go home, and I still visit a lot, when I wish I could take the old role back and see them smile by telling them that I'll get a degree or that I'll go to a Jewish singles dance. And I can dream about it, dream about them feeling good about me, but I can't ever really go back to it, because I'd always be wondering myself if I was conning them.

SHE WAS SUCKING my dick, but it was more like she was running her teeth up and down it. I touched her hair and it was crisp and fake. I couldn't touch her breasts because she was squatting down too far, and anyways to touch their breasts you gotta pay five dollars more. And I wanted to come just to get it over with, so the humiliation would be complete. Then I'll be left standing there with my pants at my ankles, a wet condom on my dick, and the whore leaving (a job done) saying see ya. And I'm in this old torn down park with dying trees only good for whores and junkies and drunks in the night. And me too. Then I walk back to my apartment sure to wash my face in the kitchen sink and brush my teeth if I'm not too lazy. Then I go to sleep but I'm not tired and I think about how my pillow case is from childhood and how I used to love sleeping on the pictures of football helmets. And I think how my mom packed it for me so I wouldn't be lonely for home in the big city. I think about these things and then I fall asleep.

IT'S TOTALED

It's funny the things we forget and then remember. I destroyed the family car three weeks after receiving my license. My friend and I took it out for a drive during school, it was our lunch hour. He was eating a bagel and between bites he said, "Let's play Starsky and Hutch." I wanted to show off my newly acquired skills so I drove between fifty-five and sixty miles per hour on a winding road where the speed limit is thirty-five.

We were having a great time, the freedom of a car was new to us, something we had longed for during seventeen years of back seat transportation. There were a couple of close calls but I miraculously and excitingly pulled us out of them. Then we came to one turn at the bottom of a treacherous and steep hill. We hit some gravel and came out of the turn too fast. I was holding on to the wheel, but I didn't even think to steer, it was too late, and we turned our heads slow to one another, I could see the very rim of his glasses, and we said together quiet and solemn 'o god.' And it took only a second, but I felt myself waiting to hit the tree. I think I closed my eyes and maybe we both screamed. I woke up slumped over the wheel.

My friend was sitting still, just staring ahead. Everything was quiet, a few things creaked. We had gone up a bank, smashed into a large tree, then rolled back facing the opposite direction. I got out of the car. The front end was cut in two, sliced by the tree. The roof was in the shape of a tent, buckled up and cracked. The passenger door had fallen off. The windshield had a thousand spider cracks. My friend stepped out.

He said, "My glasses." We began to look for his glasses, they were in a tree thirty feet away, dangling on a branch, unbroken, unscratched. He put them on. I couldn't lift my right arm.

"Are you all right?" I asked.

"I'm fine. I can't believe we're alive. How are you?"

"I can't move my arm, I think it's broken."

A telephone repairman was up a pole fixing a line. He was staring at us and holding on very tight. We could have hit his pole.

"Take the keys out," he shouted.

I took the keys out and threw them to the ground. Teachers returning from lunch hour drove past and looked at us through their windows. No one stopped.

The repairman tapped into the wire and called the police. I thought of running up the road and hitching to New York.

"My father is going to kill me," I said.

The police arrived. The cop who responded was Officer Disano, he had taught me driver safety just two months before and he knew my father from the auxiliary police squad. He looked at me, then at my father's new family car, and he said, "It's totaled," and he smiled wide under his mustache. The other cop looked inside the car and said, "What the hell happened?" I looked in the car and realized that the whole windshield and dashboard were covered with cream cheese, my friend's bagel had exploded at high speeds. The cop thought some strange bodily fluid had been forced out of us by the crash. Instead of blood my car was smeared with cream cheese.

"My friend was eating a bagel," I said.

"Were you eating a bagel while driving and lost control?"

"No."

The ambulance arrived and I began to cry out of fear and shock. They put me on a stretcher and Officer Disano helped lift me in. I said to him, "I'm sorry," and I thought my tears might help. He said, "You skidded for ninety feet. You must have been going pretty fast. I'd write you up, but I know your father will take care of you, Vine," and he shut the ambulance doors and I thought to myself, doesn't he know I'm Jewish? And I realized I was getting out of a ticket because he thought my father would beat me, yet I knew my father wouldn't hit me, he never had, he couldn't ever "take care" of me that way, but he would yell and the way he would do it would be a lot worse than a punch. So in a sense Disano was right, he just didn't know the method.

The ride to the hospital went fast and I cried the whole way there. My friend tried to joke and said, "Look at it this way, we're getting to ride in an ambulance." At the hospital they wheeled me in, stripped me down, and X-rayed my disfigured, throbbing shoulder. They put me in a room with a bed and I stared at the window across the hall. I wanted to jump out of it, but I knew that we were on the first floor. The doctor came in with the X rays and told me that my shoulder was not broken, only deeply bruised, but that I should keep my arm in a sling for at least a week. He said I could spend the night at home and a little while later my mother came to pick us up. She had borrowed a neighbor's car and she was alone, my father wasn't home yet, and she hadn't left him a note. When she came in the room I could tell that she wasn't sure if she was angry at me or grateful, my father's voice was in her head too, but she broke through her confusion and she kissed me. And in the car riding back when I said, "I'll never drive again," she told me that as soon as my arm was better, she'd have me behind the wheel.

When we were leaving the hospital my friend, who had been reading magazines and sticking his head in my room and cracking jokes, touched the side of his face, saw blood on his fingers, and fainted. They laid him down, found a little cut from glass near his ear, and stitched him up. After that we left and he was quiet and my mother drove him home and went inside with him to talk to his mother. Then we drove back to our house and pulled down the driveway. My father's company car was there and he had no idea what had happened.

I marched right down to the basement and to his office. It's behind a door and it's really a converted storage space where the boiler is and if you're tall you can't stand up fully. It's the most crowded little room I've ever seen, he's layered it like a nest with all the things he's been too fearful to throw away. He has cabinets filled with old bank books and records, and boxes filled with screws, nails, and nuts and shoe boxes filled with free pens and calendars taken from businesses. Amid all the clutter his guns and rifles hang on the walls and ceiling. I knocked at the door and went in; he was working at his desk.

"Dad?"

He turned around and saw my arm in the sling, "What happened?" Right away he was nervous and excited.

"I took the car out during lunch and hit some gravel and I skidded and went into a tree. I didn't mean to. Please don't be upset, but I think it's totaled. I'm sorry." My mother had told me to give it to him straight, so I did, everything but the Starsky and Hutch, which I never told anybody.

He screamed at me and raged for ten minutes. His eyes were furious and he kept wanting to stand up and explode, but the office was too small, so he just sat there in his chair swiveling and screaming with his hands knifing the air. He seemed like he was in pain and all I kept hearing about was money and how would he afford this and how could I have done this to him.

"I trusted you goddamnit! That car cost me nine thousand dollars. Does that mean anything to you? Or can you just throw it away like it was nothing? I try to be giving and now I can't even look at you. My father never let me drive his car. I only drove it the day he died and that was to take my mother home from the hospital. I let you drive my car and you wreck it. You're an idiot, you act like you're smart, but you're an idiot." He continued yelling as I walked out of the office and as I went up the stairs, I heard him scream, "I can't believe it," and my shoulder pounded.

I went up to my room and lay in the dark crying in my bed. Then I stopped, I knew what to do. I returned to his office. He was on the phone with my friend's parents asking them if they would sue. I took one of his handguns off the wall. He didn't see me. I went to one of his secret stashes of bullets (in case of burglars) and loaded it, just as he had taught me. I went back to the office and stood behind him silently and waited for him to finish. He hung up the phone and turned in his chair. I handed him the long, dark barreled .38.

"Dad, please shoot me."

Something came into his eyes and he hugged me and kissed me and said that he was sorry, that he was thankful I was alive, that the money didn't mean anything. I didn't believe him really, but I got what I wanted out of him and as he hugged me and cried into my neck, I looked at the gun now on the desk and I felt something shut down, I hated my father and thought I might like to shoot him.

JOY

Sometimes Joy comes on real healthy and other times it's more clear to me why she's my girl friend. When she's going good her emotions seem to be in all the right places and she talks about us dissolving barriers and communicating and loving one another. Then other times she tells me about the pills she keeps in her top drawer "just in case," and how knowing the pills are there gives her a sense of security. She says things like that and I start feeling comfortable like I'm on common ground again because then she's like all the other girls I've known, semi-suicidal. Every one of them eventually tells me some horror story of rape or molestation or incest attack or abortion or suicide attempt (Joy is the only one I've met that's had a problem with the Dalkon Shield), and I wonder to myself, what the hell is going on out there?

The latest thing Joy sprang on me was the other night she called me up and said, "Have you ever wanted to slash your face?" I took it in stride, heard the slight tone of mental insanity in her voice, and answered calmly, "Well, sometimes when I shave I think how dangerous this might be, but I've never really wanted to hurt myself in that way." I thought my calmness about the whole thing would be good, but she was silent on her end, so I said, "You don't want to, do you?" That triggered her and she shot it out in a staccato burst, "I've been thinking about it because everybody tells me how pretty I am and they think I must be O.K., they say, 'Joy you're so cute, you're so wonderful,' but I'm not so fucking cute, I'm not O.K., I'm sick inside and nobody sees it and if I slashed my face then maybe they'd notice."

I was reeling a little, but decided to play it tough, "I'm gonna see you tomorrow night and take you out for Chinese food and you better not have done anything. Can you handle that?" She was quiet for a second, then said yes, real soft. I had helped shake her out of it, the insane tone was gone, and we talked a little while longer and I soothed her just like one of those pros on the crisis line. I told her that she'd be fine, that she should go to sleep, and that we'd worry about tomorrow tomorrow. I hung up the phone and appraised my own face in the mirror, I was looking pretty good, but I wished she hadn't put any ideas in my head.

END DOORS OUT

When I get very drunk I have sex with men. History has proved this. The first time it happened I was nineteen and I was still living at home, but I got drunk in New York. It was in the Village and it must have been after midnight and I had been drinking heavily for a couple of hours. A man at the bar I was at (one of many bars that night) bought me a drink and when I finished it he asked me to come back to his place to drink some more. I didn't think it was a gay bar I was at, there were women, and so I told myself that it was fine to accept an invitation for drinks, I'd get two free ones then leave. We took a taxi to his place and I told him my name was David.

He was tall with dark hair and he was in his late thirties and later when I touched him his muscles moved and felt funny under his skin. He had a nice apartment, he seemed rich, and there was a picture of his parents on a desk and I wondered if they knew.

We had some strong drinks and he was pushy and he told me that he wanted to give me a massage. My heart was pounding and I said, "With my clothes on." So we went into his bedroom and a little while later I was sucking on his dick and he said, "You like to have a cock in your mouth." And this upset me, a fag was calling me a fag. He came in my mouth and I searched around for it with my tongue, it wasn't much, just like some thick water hidden in the well in the front of my teeth, but I didn't want to swallow it and I got out of the bedroom and spit it into the bathroom sink. That didn't seem to bother him, I guessed that a lot of guys must do that, and when I lay back down he blew me and he ate it. And then I must have slept for a while, all the drinking had caught up with me, and I was sleeping on my belly and I awoke when he had started sliding his dick along the crack of my ass and I didn't stop him. Then he turned me around and put my legs on his shoulders. He worked his penis inside me and it took a while, and all I could do was beg in a little voice, "Please, go slow, it hurts."

When he was done I went and took a shower. When I came out he was angry at me for locking the bathroom door, he had wanted to be in there with me, and I thought to myself, doesn't he realize I'm not drunk anymore? I got dressed and I asked for money for a taxi to Penn Station. I lied to him and told him that I was low on cash and that there was an early-morning train to Boston I could still make if I hurried, I told him I was from Boston. He gave me five bucks and said, "That should be more than enough." I left him and he was smoking a cigarette and when I got outside I took a taxi to Penn Station and I was glad when it only cost two bucks and change. I hadn't told him it was my first time.

I caught an early train back to New Jersey and I sat in my vinyl seat. I looked at my legs and the nice clothes I had worn into New York seemed dirty and I felt sorry for them. After we passed under the Hudson and came up in New Jersey I looked out my window and it was morning, but still dark out. I could see my reflection in the tinted glass and I tried to give a big smile, but my face, whose face? still looked sad. The conductor came for my ticket, I didn't look him in the eye, and I listened to the loudspeaker call out the strange Jersey town names, Elizabeth, Metro Park, Metuchen, Rahway, Edison. I had to use the train toilet and I looked in the bowl before I flushed. When it was my stop, I followed instructions, it seemed very important to follow instructions, and I took the end doors out.

I walked home, the sun had come up, and my mother was making eggs. It seemed incredible to me that I could return home from being fucked and my mother would still be making breakfast. My ass was burning, I had shit out the man's white sperm and I wanted to hold my mother to cry in her neck, to tell her that I had been fucked and didn't know why I let it happen. But instead I sat down and ate my breakfast, how can you tell your mother that her son feels like a daughter.

When I finished I went upstairs and lay down on my childhood bed. It was very quiet and I listened and my body was like a house and I could hear different doors slamming.

WHEN MY MOTHER *was pregnant with me John F. Kennedy was assassinated and she cried. And years later when I would watch football she would always want Dallas to lose.*

Also when she was pregnant with me she broke out in a horrible rash. Her doctors feared that she had measles. There was discussion of an abortion, because the fetus could be damaged by the disease. But my mother wanted this baby, since a year before she had a miscarriage. When she stopped a certain medication the rash went away, and they weren't sure whether it had been an allergy or the disease. In either case they did not know how the baby, how I, would turn out.

When I had my car crash a few years ago my mother came to the hospital and she didn't say much then. But the next day she came to my bedroom and she was crying. I remember now that I asked her why, and she said, "I'm crying the way I did when you were born, it's the same kind of crying. I think I'm crying to thank God."

Because my mother has said things like this to me and because of her love for me, I try never to think of her.

JIMMY WARREN

Jimmy Warren is a little bum with a broken flat nose and a sailor's stubble. I was pretending to be a writer and carrying my yellow pad and asked Jimmy if he could tell me what it's like to be a bum. He had a bum's great humility and told me a little of his story, "I was shipping out working on boats you know and doing some boxing, you'll meet a lot of bullshit artists down here saying they're ex-boxers, but I really boxed, I was a middleweight, forty-nine and two. You'd be surprised what you find down here. But mostly I was shipping out and then my son went to Vietnam, I didn't hear from him for two years or something so I called my ex-wife to find out where he was. And my brother-in-law answered the phone, I said, 'Bobby deceased?' He didn't answer, so I said, I just knew he was dead, 'Where's he buried at?' I wanted to visit the grave, she's down in Florida, but I wanted to go, my brother-in-law said, 'We had him

110

cremated.' They didn't even fucking ask me, just cremated his body, I wanted to visit his grave that damn bitch, probably too cheap to bury him. A father should be able to visit his son's grave. The brother-in-law told me that Bobby stepped on a bamboo stake that they piss and shit on, and it went right through my boy's foot and he died of an infection. So I went out, got drunk, and been drunk ever since. I started off with Johnnie Walker Red, then it was Fleischman's, then beer, and now nothing but wine. You know you get a bottle or a pack of cigarettes and I don't even see 'em coming, but there they are, three or four lined up trying to bum a smoke or drink, and I can't refuse 'em. They give me when I need it, that's the way it works, like a bunch of sea gulls."

I looked at Jimmy's hands that he rubbed together while he talked, and they were covered with green open sores that wouldn't heal, he said, "My hands are so contaminated it's disgraceful." One of his shoulders hung low and broken in a dirty sling, he had no shirt on and I could see where the joint had separated unnaturally. Jimmy told me he had staggered into the street and been hit by a van, "It was a god damn hit and run!" I then asked him how long he had been living on the street.

"I know I've been on the street ten years because I was fifty when I had a young girl living with me. She was an epileptic. I had to put her in Metropolitan Hospital for the seizures, but then she came back from the hospital and I had vodka all over the place, her eyes lit up like a Christmas tree, I said, 'Honey you don't want to touch that stuff.' But a woman can get around a man. She drank and took her epilepsy medicine. I made a mistake, I had her lay down and I kept on drinking, a neighbor came in, saw the girl, and called the cops. When they came she was dead. I didn't even know it. They put her in a canvas bag and the cop threw her over his shoulder like a sack of potatoes. I was screaming, 'What are you doing to her, what the hell you doing?' They called in homicide, thought I killed her but by then I was grieving and I didn't give a fuck if I got locked up. She was a beautiful young girl, it was an overdose of pheno-barba-tall and vodka, at that time I was fifty years old and I gave up, it was a god damn overdose, pheno-barba-tall and vodka, I didn't kill her. Now I'll be sixty, December twenty-third, ten years in the street." Jimmy put his head in his battered hands, "I can't ship out no more, I never been this bad. It's not easy down here, winter or summer, it's not easy."

I filled my yellow pad that night with Jimmy's stories and thanked him for talking and gave him fifty cents. He said, "You can interview me any time, just ask the guys where I am, they all know Jimmy Warren." Since then I keep my eye out for Jimmy, like most bums in the Bowery he'll disappear for a few days. I spotted him once passed out on some stairs, his white belly red and bruised hanging over the slate, his arm dead and useless out of the sling.

By his head were some cleaned off chicken bones and vomit. Bums usually don't eat and when they do they can't hold it, so before their liver quits they die of malnutrition. Two other bums were sitting next to Jimmy and they were humble, because like most bums the booze has squeezed out their egos.

"Jimmy all right?" I asked.

"He's all right sir."

"You going to take care of him?" I gave these fifty-year-old men a quarter each.

"Yes sir. We'll take care of him, don't worry. Thank you, sir, and god bless you." They nodded their heads to me and smiled.

I walked away and thought to myself that they really meant it when they said god bless you. I thought about that and I thought about Jimmy Warren and I felt the other coins jingle in my pocket.

HIS EYES
WERE BAD

I lost my virginity my senior year in high school.
I had a sixteen year old girl friend with brown hair
in braids and cute little tits, and I wish I had a
sixteen year old girl friend now. I think about her
when I go home and I pass the sign for her street,
but I haven't seen her in years. Sometimes I think I'll
give her a call, but she's probably not my type anymore.

We were going out for about two months and
did our making out in the car. Then a big break came
our way—her parents were going out on a Saturday
night. They told her, even though they liked me, that
I couldn't come over. So after they left she called me
and I drove over and parked the car up the block, in
case of neighbors, and went in the back door. We
made out for a while on the couch in her den and
we were going farther than ever before. And I was
counting off the bases and thinking about Ethan,

thinking maybe I could win him back, make him like me again by telling him how far I had got. Thinking of him inspired me and I made it all the way to third and I rested there awhile, until she said, "You can if you want to."

I hadn't expected to hit a home run and I just lay there stunned. She waited and squeezed my hand and I was caught in a lie. I had told her that I had slept with older girls, so that whenever she was ready (she was a virgin) I could handle it because I had experience. So she was ready and I was filled with fear and I didn't know what to do, but now was no time to get honest. I forced myself into action and I whispered to her, "I want to." I pulled my underwear off, got my penis out, lay on top of her, poked it around a bit, and then went soft. After having an erection for the last hour, and the last four years, my penis died at the most crucial moment of my young life and my heart was breaking. I was pushing it against her and it was bending in half and receding to the point of vanishing, and I was hoping she wouldn't know the difference. I was moving around as much as I could, trying everything, rubbing this way and that, but nothing helped. I was hating myself and it seemed like my father was right behind me yelling "Klutz!" like he had done my whole life. I kept on pushing and praying and almost crying, almost thought I would quit, and then God came through and it got hard and slipped in there like I had been doing it my whole life. And I think my whole soul just gave a big smile and I thought to myself, this is all I want to do from now on. I just held myself in there and didn't even move, my eyes were closed and I was proud. Then she moved like a woman can, to take in a little bit more, and she made a noise, a sigh, and maybe she raised her hips just the slightest, and I was overwhelmed by her presence and the urge to come, and I panicked, yanked it out, and went on her belly. I had lasted ten seconds and she was sixteen and there was a look on her face, and I never wanted to have sex again.

She got up and held her panties to her stomach so the sperm wouldn't run off and she looked like she was going to cry. I heard her say, not really to me, "I can't believe it," and she went out of the room and up the stairs. It had turned out bad and I just sat there, but I was already working it around in my head, shaping the story up, so that I could make it sound good for Ethan and other guys. I went to the bathroom and when I was pissing I saw her father's eyeglasses on the sink. I got scared for a second thinking that maybe he was in the house, but I knew he wasn't. I liked her father, he was big and confident and Protestant. He thought I was too, she hadn't told them I was Jewish, and that was fine with me. He was very nice to me and one time when I was waiting for her to get ready, he and I had watched some sports together on TV, and I had never even done that with my own father. So I put

those wire glasses on and I looked in the mirror,
but I couldn't see much because his eyes were bad.
I put the glasses back on the sink and I thought
of stealing them or bending them in the middle,
but I didn't do it, I figured he would know it
was me.

LOOKING FOR
THE ANSWERS

It was one of those days when every time I went to go out the door, something grabbed me in the back of the brain and said, lie down and masturbate one more time. So I spent the whole day moving in and out of consciousness between naps and reveries, counting the hours until the free phone-sex message would change. It changes three times a day. Finally around midnight when the paper bag to my right was filled with tissue paper I pushed myself out the door with a surge of will and courage.

Once on the street the cold air braced me and I judged myself guilty of murdering a perfectly good day off and so sentenced myself to walk as far as I could to make up for the terrible sloth I had just endured. I didn't stop, except for an onion roll at an all-night deli, until one A.M., when I arrived at Penn Station. I was not alone in the great train cave under Thirty-fourth Street as there were hundreds of homeless snuggled into corners to sleep or grow ill. I walked around and all was yellow down there because of the lights, except for some drunk sports fans who seemed green and waited for trains to New Jersey. An occasional cop patrolled with his modern-handled billy club to keep all of us in order and I always think cops are fat, until I remember the bulletproof vests under their blue shirts.

I sat down on the escalator stairs and perched above me, beside me, and below me, like so many birds in a tree were old bag ladies cooing and chirping to themselves and shaking their saggy, gray faces in imaginary conversations. Some of them drifted in and out of sleep and their heads fell to their chests, until they would snap them back, afraid and alert. They muttered to themselves to stay awake to protect their bags. They're known to carry money or something of value in those sacks, and to fall asleep might mean a kick to the ribs (and their bones heal no more) and the loss of another possession. So they sit alone fighting sleep and they are all loners, for unlike the fellowship that exists among male bums, the bag ladies don't even trust one another.

I offered the old lady next to me half the roll I had bought at the deli. She accepted it, gummed half of it, then wrapped the rest in some old sandwich paper and hid it somewhere in her many layers of clothes. I watched her closely, because over the years I've had this off and on fantasy that someone out there is carrying a pearl of knowledge that is meant just for me. It's something of a wise man search and I don't take it too seriously, but I have made a point of talking to lots of people, whores, bums, countermen, relatives, yet no one has told me, as far as I can tell, the thing I need to hear. So having given this bag lady something to eat, I thought that perhaps she wouldn't mind giving me some advice. Maybe she was the one.

"Excuse me, ma'am. I was wondering, if you don't mind, if you could tell me . . . See I'm cracking up," I blurted out, "I mean I am very unhappy, I spent the whole day in my room, and I don't know what to do. Do you have any idea?" As with every time I ask this question I experience this wonderful eternal moment of hope that *the* answer is coming forth. She was a fiery one and went right into it, almost yelling at me.

"What do you expect. Of course you're unhappy. I'm unhappy, we're all unhappy because the god damn Jews killed our Christ. You know that, everyone knows that, and not only did they kill Christ but they're still out here doing evil because they took all my money, took all my clothes, turned my children against me and put me on the street. They'd have me sell myself, but I will not sell my body. And they're starving us and feeding their god damn Jewselves. Just look at all these Christians starving and sleeping on cardboard. You don't see any Jews down here. And a Jew owns Penn Station, you better believe it! I hate the bastards."

She stopped a second, took a breath, and her eyes got a little less wild. She ran her hands over the gray, dirty clump of weed that was her hair just like a genteel lady. She smiled with her gums at me and the gray skin of her face creased and shifted upward. She was calm.

"I can see you're a good boy," she said, "you must have fine parents. I can tell these things. They must have told you, to be happy you've got to have a position. With a position you can do anything, have food, money, a house. You see," she smiled again and explained, "I don't have a position. I'm trying to get one, but I don't have it yet. But you're young, get yourself a position and the money hungry Jews won't put you on the street."

"I'm a Jew," I said.

She turned her head quickly in shock to look at me and said, "And you don't have a position?"

*I SAID TO my father once, "I can't stand the
way you eat." But that didn't stop him. The last time
I was home I was talking to my mother at the kitchen
table and he came in to the room and said, "I'm
hungry." He expected to be fed, expected like a baby
bird holding its membranous pink head up and beak
open to have food put in his mouth.*

*So she got up to get him something, he doesn't
know how to do it for himself, and I went up to my
room and shut myself in. But I could hear him chewing up the flight of stairs and through my closed door.
I could hear him chewing as if he was right beside
me, those sounds, and I sat at my desk, then threw
myself onto my bed and covered my head with my
pillow until he was done.*

*Then he came up the stairs and into my room.
He didn't know I was half-dying because of disgust
for him and he said, "I want a hug. I'm lachry-
mose." That's a new word for him and I got off the
bed and I held him. I kept my hips back so we
wouldn't touch below the waist and he put his face
in my shoulder. He might have been crying a little
and I turned my head to the right so his hair wouldn't
go in my mouth.*

MITZVAH

Aunt Doll called me and said I should do a *mitzvah* every day. She says that she helps a blind boy in front of Alexander's. She brings him coffee in a glass jar and solicits the rich Jewish ladies to give him money by waving them over and giving them a guilty nod with her head.

"He's out there from ten in the morning till six and if I didn't give him food, a little tuna fish, he wouldn't eat. He's Italian and his name is Juliano, I call him Julie. One of the ladies asked me if he was my son, and I said no, but that I'd be proud to have a son like that. He's blind."

Aunt Doll never had children, she had a hysterectomy when she was nineteen and my mother is her niece, but more like a daughter, so I'm like a grandson. And she's always loved me the most because I'm a redhead like her. She told me that if people said nice things about my hair I should spit three times and say a *cunnahurra* in case they were giving me the evil eye. She says that her problem in life is that she got too many evil eyes that she didn't know about. But she says the best prevention against an evil eye working is to do a *mitzvah* every day. She told me I could do one if I helped the old ladies with their bags at the supermarket, especially now that winter was coming on. So I decided to try but none of them would let me. They're all old Italian ladies where I shop at the Super T-Bone Market on Mott Street and they leave with their plastic bags of food wrapped around their wrists and it cuts off the circulation to their hands and I hate the way that looks. Their ankles are already terribly swollen and they have thick shoulder muscles from years of working hard. Most of them have outlived their husbands.

I asked this one lady if I could help her and I think she cursed me in Italian and she had lots of little brown skin tags under her eyes. After that I decided to quit trying to do *mitzvahs* and I went outside. I went across the street and I was floundering in front of Parisi's bakery staring at the fresh rolls and my breath was fogging up the window a little because it was chilly out. When I turned around the old lady who cursed me came out of the market and just as I looked at her a Hispanic kid went running by screaming and the old lady tipped over. It doesn't take much to disturb an old lady's machinery and she lay on her back with her arms spread out like a fallen angel. Somehow the plastic bags were still twisted closed and locked to her wrists. Her dress lifted a little and I could see how the stockings were bunched at the top and how they wrapped around her mid-thigh like a tourniquet. I was worried that I had given her the evil eye by mistake and I rushed to her and as gently as I could I rolled her to the edge of the street and with her feet hanging over the sidewalk she was able to stand by pushing down on the road. She was a little stunned and she let me walk her back to her building which was only two blocks away in the heart of Little Italy on Grand Street. We didn't talk the whole way there and I carried the food and when we got to her door I noticed some mudlike blood leaking out of her stocking near her right knee. She dug her key out of her coat pocket and took out a change purse. She was about to give me money and I said, "No, thank you," and I put down her groceries and I ran away. I ran all the way back to my room and called Aunt Doll to tell her I had just done a *mitzvah*, but she wasn't in, she was probably with Juliano.

MOVIE STAR

My friend called the other night and said, "Alexander do you want to go shopping?" It was after midnight and I wasn't doing anything, so I answered, "Sure, I'll go along for a ride." I like to call him the gentleman shopper, but really his name is Adam, and he's Jewish like me, so we get along fine. Thirty minutes after he called he was outside my building honking on the horn of his 1978 blue Dart. I hustled down the stairs, got in the car, and shook his hand. I hadn't seen him for a while and he was nicely dressed and had a big smile on his face, but he looked terrible. He lives with his parents and they persecute him and he works in his father's rug business, so his nerves are shot. His stomach is no good and his hair is thinning prematurely. He's not the prettiest guy to look at, but I don't mind really because all we do together is cruise for whores and you don't have to be beautiful for that.

We drove over to the Lincoln Tunnel at a good clip and I could tell he was anxious to get over there, he hadn't had his fix of whores in a while. We cruised up and down Eleventh and Tenth avenues between Thirty-third and Forty-fourth streets as sort of a warm up and just window shopped the scattered collection of whores on the corners. Other than the girls there's not much to see in this part of town, except old warehouses and gigantic signs giving instructions on how to enter the tunnel. We watched the whores do their thing—wave at cars and smile, crook a finger to call you over, flash a tit, and lean inside the car window and say, "Lookin' for a date honey?" And we just drove up and down, he wasn't ready to pick one yet, and we both kept a hand in our pockets to jiggle our hard-ons.

We were driving for about fifteen minutes and listening to jazz on the radio. It was a Benny Goodman special and it was a cold night and the heater was blowing along with the music. I love Benny Goodman, but whenever I looked at my friend's face I felt my mood slip and I felt myself getting cranky. I began to realize that he hadn't stopped smiling the whole time I was with him and it was a smile I didn't like. His lips were pulled back tight and his big teeth were sticking out and his eyes were all glazed and euphoric. I'd seen him get this way once before when we went to one of those places on Seventh Avenue where you buy a girl a drink that costs you fifteen bucks and she talks to you for ten minutes. I didn't get a girl, but just sat there and sipped a soda water, while he dished out sixty bucks' worth of drinks to talk to a petite but busty Dominican girl. He sat there holding her hand for almost an hour and he had the same expression on his face as he did now in the car. It upset me to see him like that again, so I started putting him down to make myself feel better.

"Why are you so happy? You think these pretty whores are waiting for you? Do you think they like you or something?"

"I don't know, some of them do. I don't think they'd do it if they didn't like it. A couple of them said I have nice eyes and nice skin. You know they think white men are good looking because of the color difference. Some of them have told me I was handsome."

I had heard it before and after he made his little speech I let him have it. "When are you going to realize that they don't like doing it and they don't like doing it with you? All you are is another man with a ten-dollar bill who needs to come because he can't find a woman to do it for free."

The smile came off his face and suddenly I felt bad for wrecking his big night out. I was wrong to lace into him, a man can never hear sense when you're talking about his addiction, and my friend's addiction was whores. So I decided to change gears and not be cranky, even if I had to fake it. I tried to get him back into a good mood and it wasn't too hard. I spotted two whores on the corner of Thirty-ninth.

"Look at the legs on the one on the right. Do you want her? Pull over if you want her, she looks sexy as hell."

"No, not her. I want to get one that I really like."

"Well, she's out here and we'll find her. We'll spot a beauty that will be perfect for what you want tonight."

That seemed to cheer him up and the smile came back a little and we kept on driving up and down the avenues. There were plenty of girls out, they tend to cluster in groups of three and four on the different corners, and they all looked sexy, but you have to have a fine eye, because some of them that look good through the car window are a pretty tough sight up close in your front seat. If you're not careful you'll get a husky voiced transvestite, but unless you're particular it doesn't really matter.

Finally, he spotted one that he wanted, he said, "Look at her! O my God, that's the one I want, she's a movie star!" It was a white one in good condition, which is rare, the only white girls on the street are usually end of the line junkies who don't have long to live. But this one was for real and she was also on the other side of Eleventh Avenue, so we had to floor it down Thirty-sixth to the West Side Highway and then back up Thirty-seventh. He drove as fast as he could over the potholed streets and I held on, but when we got up to the corner she was climbing into some car with Jersey plates.

We drove around some more waiting for her to

finish and when she was left off at another corner, we just missed her again. She was the most popular whore on the street, white, young, and beautiful, and as soon as she was let out of one car another one scooped her up. We missed her one more time, it was hard to guess where she'd be left off next, and then she disappeared for more than a half hour. Somebody probably wanted something more than a blow job, but if she was a good whore it probably wouldn't even go in her vagina. They have a way of sitting on you and putting it in their ass cheeks and squeezing to fool you that it's the real thing. It saves them wear and if a guy does notice he's probably too nervous and ashamed to say anything.

So we were driving and waiting and he was getting more and more frantic. He kept on saying, "Where is she? Where is she?" And then after about twenty minutes the sick gleam went out of his eyes, and his shoulders relaxed, and he said, "I want to go home." I could have let him quit, he had never done that before, but I had been sitting in that car too long and I wanted to be entertained. I started sweet-talking him into driving a little bit longer, that any minute now she would show up and it would be worth it. I kept him going for a while telling him how pretty she was and then I told him that if she didn't show up in five minutes we'd leave and just as I said it we saw her on the corner and we were the first car there.

He rolled down his window and she did the talking. "You wanna blow job?" He nodded yes, he was speechless, and she said, "O.K., but I won't do it with your friend in the car. No free shows." That was fine with me, she knew there were crazies in New York, and I respected that, so she and I traded places, the front seat for the street. This gave me a chance to check her out close, she was a big, full-limbed American girl, with long brown hair and a pretty face. She was probably a runaway and seventeen, but with all the makeup she looked thirty. I closed the car for her like the smooth doorman that I am and I told him I'd wait on the corner. They drove off to find a quiet, deserted parking lot.

I went and leaned against an old warehouse on the corner of Forty-first. A couple of whores approached me at once and I told them I wasn't interested (I didn't feel like spending the money) and one of them gave me the finger and another said, "Get out of here boy, you're gonna wreck our business, are you a cop or a queer?" Luckily some cars pulled up and they left me alone. I watched them do their job, the girls were coming and going, and they were even working across the street where a couple of Greyhound buses were parked. The drivers come down three blocks from the Port Authority for a quick lay before going on some long haul. I was taking it all in, but after a while I was getting cold and I started thinking that my friend had been gone longer than the usual ten minutes the whole process takes. I was wondering what might have happened, some whores carry knives or mace, and then one of the whores who had approached me before, an old-timer with a gold wig, had come back and was pointing at me. She started laughing and called to the others.

"Hey girls look who's still here. What ya lookin' at boy? Trying to figure out how it's done? Why don't you find out? Get your pants off and get to work! Let's pimp him, somebody give me a dress!"

She was laughing wildly and the other whores joined in. But before I was stripped down, made up, and had a wig slapped on my head, and turned into a whore (and God knows I might've enjoyed the change) my friend pulled up. The movie star stepped regally out and I quickly got in. I was excited by the whole thing, but I was relieved to get out of there, and relieved to see that he was in one piece. We headed back downtown and he was quiet and I was curious as to how it went.

"C'mon tell me, how was the movie star?"

"To be honest, she wasn't that good, you know, with her teeth, but she was pretty. And she really is an actress."

"I can't believe that. How much did it cost?"

He hesitated, then said, "Thirty-five." He was embarrassed and knew that it was way too much. They all start out saying thirty-five, then you work them down to ten or fifteen. They say thirty-five to catch the occasional timid first-timer who doesn't know the prices, but he was experienced. I couldn't understand how it happened.

"You couldn't get her lower?"

"No."

I couldn't understand this, so I said, "She probably charges more because she's white," and then I added, "and what took so long anyway?"

His lips started trembling, the strain of the whole night was getting to him. He was on the verge of tears and he started talking, the confession came forth.

"I paid thirty-five and I didn't even try to get her lower because I liked her. But it took so long because I couldn't come. That's the first time that happened. Everything had been going great, after all the driving I was so excited and I started running my fingers through her hair, it was so beautiful, but when I did that she stopped and looked up at me like I was sick and she yelled at me, 'Don't mess up my hair, don't touch it.' Like I was disgusting or something. I lost my erection and she tried to get me going but the mood was killed. I didn't know what to do with my hands, I held them in the air, and then she gave up and said, " 'You can't come? I knew you were weird, take me back.' I can't believe it, I mean what's the point if you can't touch their hair, I mean what's the point?"

I felt bad for him and I tried to convince my hand to get over there and touch his shoulder, but I just couldn't do it. We drove to my street in silence and he and I both knew that in a way it was all my fault. When he pulled up in front of my door I got out of the car and we didn't say goodbye and he was gone before I had my key out of my pocket.

I went and sat on my stoop and it was cold out, but I wasn't ready to go in, so I lifted my right pants leg and ran my fingers along my shin and felt the nicks in the bone where I got kicked playing soccer fifteen years ago. I was sitting there and sort of hoping that somebody I knew would walk by, but it was almost three o'clock and I don't know many people. I looked down to Grand Street to see if Goldie was on the corner, I've looked down there for months, but she hasn't come back to this part of town, and I don't know where she is. When I was done with my shin and when I was cold enough, I went up to my room and called it a night.

LITTLE FINLAND

Joy and I found a small bar called Little Finland. We went in there and had one beer each and I noticed the jukebox and when I went to look at it all the songs were Finnish. I put in a few quarters and polka-like music came out and I took Joy's hand and we started to dance in small circles around the wooden tables. And it was a beat-up place with a long bar and two pool tables in the back. There was one old drunk looking at the TV over the liquor and there was a couple of big ugly drunks playing pool. I think we were the first people ever to dance there. I held her close and I kept our arms rigid and bent and I whispered to her. I pretended that I was a Finnish soldier back from some brutal three year war and she, my wife-to-be three years ago and the daughter of a respected landowner, had thought I died, and so was getting married to a wealthy educated boy, and I had arrived the night of the wedding and it was the big party dance and I was still in my dirty uniform and she had been shocked to see me, they all had been shocked, and I had asked her to dance and I held her. I whispered to her in a mock Finnish accent how I wanted to make love to her one last time, for the first time, before she went to her conjugal bed. I told her how I almost died in the war and how my right leg had withered from infection but that I had never lost hope that I would see her again. And I told Joy to cry and beg and to tell me that it was too late to break off the marriage and I only held her tighter. I was believing my role and the music was wonderful, we glided across the floor, and the pool players had stopped to watch us. The largest one, an enormous staggering fellow, came over after the third song and asked, "Can I have a dance?" And I whispered to Joy that it was her groom-to-be and now was the time to forget money and land and her parents and to run away with me for forever. So we ran out of Little Finland and the drunk at the bar turned to look, and we ran on the street and when we were safe we stopped, and I was still in my role and I kissed her.

SNOWSTORM

It was snowing, but I didn't let any go in my mouth, and I hid in bars drinking and ended up drunk at Uncle Charlie's on Greenwich Avenue. The booze was making me happy and I laughed at some boys kissing, boys wearing St. Joseph High School varsity sport jackets. A muscular Latino guy watched me laugh and he gave me the eye and after a few minutes of the eye he came over and bought me a drink and I let him, but I wouldn't dance with him. We talked for a while and I noticed that my hands were waving and I looked at my fingers and they seemed very slender and feminine in their gesticulations; I wrapped them around glasses of rum and Coke, I put them in my hair, I touched his arm, and his name was Juan-Antonio and when he asked me back to his place I said yes.

While we walked there he told me that he was very healthy and I figured that was the new line, I hadn't been with a man in a while, and I told him I was healthy too and we got that out of the way and the snow was still coming down and my feet were getting wet. As soon as we got to his little place and our jackets were off, he grabbed me right away from behind and started pressing against me and running his hands up under my shirt. I squeezed my elbows down and said, "Not yet, I want a drink." So we had drinks on his little couch and he had very dark hair and he tried to kiss me and I turned my head, I felt our stubbles clash and I didn't like that. And he started undoing my pants and I kept resisting, but he was strong and his eyes weren't mean, so I gave in, it's what I wanted. But his hands once free were fast, too fast, on my breasts, on my belly, in my underwear, in my pubes. I stood up, I was drunk, "Too much," I said and I got past him, but he had yanked down my pants and underwear, and so my legs were bound, I couldn't walk, he got me from behind, squeezed my hips, I started hopping away, we were like a caboose, I said, "Where's the bedroom?"

Our clothes were off in no time and we rolled around a bit and I felt his dick brush against my thighs, and I was excited to be with somebody else who had a penis and he said he wanted to be inside me. I asked him if he had a condom and he said he did. So I put my face in his pillow and my ass in the air and I closed my eyes. My head spun a little from the booze, but I was ready. He spread some cream in my ass and worked a finger or two in there. Then his dick started knocking around and my ass was fighting letting it in and the few times I've done it in the beginning there's always been pain, but if you get through that then it starts to feel good, and you forget that it ever hurt until he tries to take it out and then your body won't let it go. And Juan-Antonio kept pushing and I tried to take deep breaths and just open up my whole body, it was almost religious, and finally he slid in there and there was no more fight. My whole ass was filled with him and his hands dug into my sides and held me there while he worked it back and forth and I opened more and more. He started to pick up speed and lay flat on my back and he lunged again and again with his dick. And I started pressing my hips back to meet him to get all of it, and I loosened my hand from the corner of the bed where I was holding on and my shoulder was driven down, but I reached back to touch it, to feel it go in me, and I held his balls and when the penis came out, I held it and there was no condom. Suddenly I didn't want to be fucked anymore and I stopped my hips and I didn't feel very drunk, I started to beg, "Pull out, pull out, please pull out." And he wouldn't, he only screwed me harder and I kept begging and finally he yanked it out and ground it into the bottom of my spine and came up my back and landed heavy on me and spread his come between us.

He rolled off and lay with his hands behind his head. And I counted to sixty to let some time pass and then I asked, "Why didn't you use a condom?"

And he said, "We were going too fast and I didn't want to stop, but it doesn't matter I pulled out in time." I said, "Are you sure? You don't think you dripped a little did you? If you drip a little that's all it takes. But it was safe right? Right?"

He got out of bed, he was angry, I had spoiled it, he said, "If you were afraid you shouldn't have come back with me," and he went out of the room. I should have dressed and left then, but I lay there and I listened to him urinate and I convinced myself that he had pulled out in time and that everything would be all right. And I didn't leave there because I wanted more sex and I had nowhere else to go, it was too late to start all over. He came back in the room with a bottle of rum, he didn't stay angry for long, and we passed it back and forth and my drunkenness which had been slipping away came back to life. We sat across from each other Indian style and after we drank a while he took a small, two-inch brown bottle out of his dresser drawer. He undid the cap and gave me the little bottle and told me to inhale its fumes. It was amyl nitrate he said and I held the bottle under my nostril and breathed in and my whole body rushed and he took my penis and started to suck and it grew hard in his mouth. The fumes out of the bottle made my heart swell and made me want to come like nothing else, but it only lasted for three-second jolts so I held the bottle to my nostril nonstop while he sucked and sucked and swallowed my whole penis. I was an immediate addict to the amyl nitrate and I wanted to come terribly and time it with a hit of the drug and so I took a giant snort and in my zeal the liquid at the bottom of the bottle poured into my nose and down my throat. It was a swift, overwhelming nausea and I knocked him off me with my leg and I ran blind into the bathroom and fell to my knees. I held on to the toilet and I vomited and somehow I didn't strangle. When I was done I collapsed and my legs spasmed and swam on the floor. I was blacking out every few seconds, I was sure I was going to die, and once when I looked up Juan-Antonio was nude above me in the doorway and I managed to grab a corner of the door and slam it shut. I vomited again and I hung my head over the bowl and I held on which helped me against the spinning and I realized I couldn't breathe through my nose. Juan-Antonio stuck his head back in and I yelled at him drunk, "My nose is damaged," and he left me alone, he closed the door.

I got up from the toilet and I turned on the shower. I was too weak to stand, so I sat in the tub and let the water beat down on me. I think I slept a bit and when I woke I thought it was water, but it was blood coming out of my nose, and I got some on my fingers and it was red but when the water came it turned brown and disappeared. I held a wash cloth to my nostrils and I hid my penis between my legs and the water pelted my bush, which has an orange color, I inherited that from my mother. And in time I got out of the shower and my fingers were crinkled and white and boiled and the bleeding had stopped. I dried myself off.

I went to the bedroom and got dressed. Juan-Antonio was still nude and he had finished the rum and he was very quiet. My shoes were still wet and I headed for his door and he walked alongside me and gave me a piece of paper with his phone number on it. He tried to hug me goodbye, but I slipped away into the hall and he didn't follow me out and I walked down the three flights of stairs to the little lobby. I put his number in my pocket and I got outside and it was cold and I had a long walk back to the Bowery. The snow had stopped and I told myself to just look at my feet and before I'd know it I'd be home. I had to breathe with my mouth and I was able to manage, but at the time it did seem sad to me that my nose didn't work anymore.

JOY WAS RUBBING my back and suddenly I had my first memory—my mother was rubbing my back in the same way and we were sitting in the white rocking chair in my room. It was dark, she was holding me to her shoulder, the crib was to my right, the door to my left, and I came to and I knew at that moment that I was alive and that I had a mother and I've remembered almost everything since. It started in that chair, rocking, rubbing, and me staring at the hall light through the crack of the door. I remember that my mother was tired and beautiful, that her hair was long, and that I was loved and held. And I remember as I got older she would sing to me before I slept and I made up the rule that if I made a noise she'd have to start again. So I'd make lots of noises, I didn't want her to leave me. I can still sing the song in my head, I sing it in a whisper the way she did.

I was thinking about all this and Joy was rubbing my back and after a while I asked for her breasts and she gave them to me and she held me. Later, when she wanted me to be a man, I didn't say it, but I didn't want to, though part of me wanted to, and I wished that just her breasts could be enough for us. I squeezed her nipple and I said, "Does that hurt?" I wanted it to, but she said no.

BETTER WITH GIRLS

When Ethan and I were fifteen we started drinking beer together. I remember the first time that we snuck out two and we went to the other side of the lake and drank them really slow while hidden in the woods. I remember we kept asking each other, "Are you drunk yet? Do you feel anything?"

We didn't like to fish or swim as much anymore, all we started caring about was how we'd get our hands on more beer. One weekend Ethan's parents went away and we managed to get a whole case. I told my parents that I was going to stay over Ethan's house which is something I had done for years. We drank the beer on the back porch and as we got drunk we kept on saying how beautiful the lake was. We drank as much as we could out of his father's tall beer glasses until we both thought we were going to be sick and Ethan pulled out the sofa bed in the big room and we both lay down and passed out.

I slept awhile and when I woke I took my clothes off. Ethan had already done the same and he was asleep on the sheets in his underwear. I was still drunk, but I didn't feel sick and I looked out the sliding windows to the lake and I thought of waking Ethan and telling him that we should go swimming. He woke on his own and I can still remember him turning his head to look at me and by accident his foot touched my leg and then the accident got bigger and we held one another. I had never touched another person, I had never kissed a girl, and Ethan rolled us over and lay on top of me. For a moment I did nothing, I wondered why I was on the bottom, but then it seemed to make sense, Ethan had always been bigger than me, and I put my arms around my friend's back, I put my face into his neck.

The next day we were hung over and tried to sweat it out by playing basketball. We had woken in the morning and said almost nothing. After one game of basketball we sat in the shade near his driveway and I was going to ask him if we could go inside and try it again, I wanted to. But before I spoke he did, he said, "Let's forget what happened last night. We were drunk and it was a bad mistake. Don't ever tell anybody. I had thought about it before, about trying it, but now I know I don't like it, it'll be a lot better with girls."

I didn't say anything to Ethan and we played another game of basketball and we never talked about it again. Our friendship returned to just about normal, except I wish that we had never found beer, because we really didn't have to talk anymore. All we did together was drink and wait till we'd got our licenses and make plans about what we'd do with our cars. And for those two years of waiting I was always trying to work up the courage to ask him if I could touch him, but I was always too scared, and then I started getting a girl friend here and there and it wasn't on my mind as much.

Ethan was the first to get his license and his parents bought him a beautiful new car. We were seventeen and everything was supposed to start happening for us, but that's when Ethan began to leave me. It started slow and it was never spoken, but he never called me first anymore and he didn't return all my calls, I was the one always phoning him. And I'd be walking to his house sometimes and he'd be pulling out of the driveway and the car would be full with people that I didn't know and I'd turn around and act like I forgot something and pray that he wouldn't see me in his rearview mirror. Somehow fourteen years of friendship could die in just one moment and I didn't know how to ask him why.

He would see me every now and then and he would act as if nothing was wrong and I couldn't believe that he didn't notice. And then this one time when we did go out, early in the night he said he was tired and wanted to go home. He dropped me off and I smiled like I always did at him, like we were still best friends, but I knew he was lying. I went into my house and I tried to sleep, but it was no good. And I couldn't tell my parents what was happening, I was embarrassed and scared to tell anyone that I was losing my best friend. So I got my bike out that night, I had destroyed the car I could use, and I cycled the half block to Ethan's house and his car wasn't there, and I knew where he was. I had seen this one boy with him just once and I didn't trust him and I knew where he lived and I rode my bike there. It was a few miles away and when I found the house Ethan's car was in front. I hid myself in the shadows of a tree and I wanted to break the car's windshield, I wanted to smash every shiny panel, I wanted to cut apart the insides with a knife, and I wanted to sit in that car till Ethan came out, and I wanted him to like me again. And too I wanted to go in the boy's house and take a baseball bat to the whole thing (I often wanted to do that to my own house) and I wanted to look at Ethan's face and I wanted to yell at him, "I knew you were lying." But all I did was turn around on my bike and swallow everything and seal it inside me. All over my body, in my lower back, in my hands, in my stomach, along the shelf of my hips, in my arms, are bags and boxes of hates and angers, and that night in front of the boy's house is down there somewhere, making little cancers maybe, but it's closed tight for now. Though that first night it leaked a little while I rode my bike and punished my legs on the hills and hated my town and hated all the ugly houses.

Yet Ethan and I never fought. I saw him less and less frequently, but we still went to an occasional movie or diner and I never told him once how I felt. It went on like that for a year and a half and I always thought it would change, that one day in the same way that it somehow had disappeared, it would come back and we'd be best friends again. So I hung on to whatever time he gave me and when you're wrapped up in it you think you're floating, but really I was just drowning more. When we were eighteen and a half his family moved and I thought that friends like Ethan and I would have a big goodbye, but all that happened was a hug and me saying that I'd write. And I wrote for a couple of years and only once did I get a letter back. So for seven years now I've walked around our neighborhood and I rowed in the boat and I methodically worked at putting it all together. I walked up and down the field, I stared at his backyard, I stared at the basketball hoop that the new people never took down, I stared at the rock in the woods (the elephant rock because it was big) that we used to climb on. And as much as I looked, it seemed that my whole childhood didn't happen because Ethan had left me at the end of it. I felt robbed that the happiness that I thought I felt was maybe unreal. And then it started to come clear to me that Ethan couldn't have woken up one day when we were seventeen and decided to leave me, he had to have been planning it all along. It took me a few years, but I began to see that he had probably hated me for almost as long as he had known me. I saw in my own behavior that in subtle, mean ways I had caused Ethan to detest me. I began to remember all the times I was cruel, how I laughed when his older brother beat him, how I laughed when he was injured. But Ethan had no other friends and he worked an incredible deception for many years, waiting for the time when he would be strong enough not to need me at all and to finally be free of me. I had loved him, but I didn't know how to love, and so he had always hated me and when he was ready he left me. And he was right to do it.

BE A DOCTOR

The killer is upon me, I'm back from the clinic, and I know I will have AIDS. The results will be ready in four weeks and I look in the mirror and say whose eyes are those? But I know my mind for the first time in my life—I've never believed that I would die. I've never even believed anybody else has died. I sat by my Grandfather's death bed and they couldn't sew his stomach back together (my father said his belly was like Swiss cheese, the flesh was so rotten) and they had a catheter stuck in his ancient dick. He was rotted out like I'm going to be, and I remember the blood dripping out of the plastic pipe in his throat into the machine that hummed alongside the wall. It sounded like a factory. And I would clean the stuff he spit out of his mouth, all the relatives thought I was so brave, but I didn't want to leave his bedside, I was praying for him to die while I was sitting there. I wanted to see it, I wanted to know it. But he kept on opening his painful blue eyes and he was sunken under the sheets and once he had a great alcoholic belly. So they had wet compresses where his stomach used to be to keep him together.

I asked him what I should do with my life. I don't know if he did, but he should have hated me—his seventy-two years are coming to an end, and I'm begging for some last words of wisdom. I've always only cared about myself, even then. And he couldn't speak, so I said, "Should I be a lawyer?" And he barely nodded his head. I was nice, I asked a question he could answer. I didn't know what else I could be, though, that's all I ever heard in my sweet Jewish family, "Be a doctor, be a lawyer."

So this nice, Jewish boy went to the clinic and before they take your blood they talk to you about the disease and the doctor said, "Let me put it bluntly, were you fucked?" And I said yes, and he explained that infected sperm can enter little cuts and tears in the anus and that I could be pregnant with AIDS. And I remember the first time I was fucked, how I closed my eyes tight and put them in the pillow, but the man wouldn't let me hide and he turned me around, put my legs on his shoulders, and said, "I want to see your face, pretty boy." So now I'm going to die, and I guess I won't be a lawyer, but I don't believe it. My grandfather died during the night and I didn't see him go.

A FULL HEAD
OF HAIR

I was wearing the thick brown coat that they let me use in the winter and when I'd leave the warmth of the double doors to get a taxi my whistle was like ice in my mouth. The restaurant was slow and I hustled for every tip I could. I stood on the corner of Park Avenue and I wondered how much freezing a face could take.

At the end of the night I counted my money as always in the coat room. In my right pocket I stuff all the ones and in the left pocket I put the spare change and the big tips from watching the regulars' Mercedeses. In the wad of ones I found a ten, somebody slipped it to me for just opening a door or getting a taxi and I hadn't even noticed. I didn't make a lot that night, but that secret ten-dollar bill made me feel like it was worth it. I was glad that somebody out there was like that.

I put my doorman's hat in my cubby and took

out the long black scarf that Aunt Doll made for me a couple of years ago and wrapped that around my head. I don't know what she did to it but that scarf keeps expanding each year and it's really like a shawl now. I wrap it around my shoulders, then over my head, and when I clutch it at the chin just my nose sticks out and a little bit of my red hair. I look like a Rabbi.

I took the subway home that cold night and I talked to myself and nobody bothered me. It's about a fifteen-minute ride to the Bowery and I got off at Spring Street station and walked in the middle of the road so that no one could jump me, but the quarters like always clanged in my pockets like bells for criminals. It's dark and quiet down here at night and you don't see anybody until you're right on top of them, but like always I made it home safe—I have never been touched. I think it's the way I move my head.

At my door there was a bum on my stoop drinking wine and his clothes looked frozen and stiff, but his face was alive and red with broken, thin veins spiderwebbed all over just beneath the skin. I tried to step around him and he said, "Are you drunk?" And I said, "No, drunk on work." He said, "That's good, that's what you're made for," then he said, "I won't bother nobody, I just wanna sip my wine." I stopped a second and looked down the street to see if the whores were out, but it was even too cold for them and when I looked back down at the bum he dropped his bottle, and his head fell not too hard onto the concrete stairs. I got my door open and took him by the shoes, I didn't want to touch his clothes or skin, and I dragged him into the little dirty space at the bottom of the inside stairs beneath the mailboxes. I closed the front door and the cold was kept out. I looked down at him and he had a full head of hair and this always astounds me. I started up to my room and I thought of putting a quarter in his pocket like the man who had given me the ten, but I couldn't do it, I couldn't part with one cent that night, I wanted it to stay whole, I wanted to count it in the morning.

HOME

I was going home to have a Friday night dinner with my parents. I wasn't going to tell them that I had gone for the test and was waiting for my results, but I sort of wanted to be around them anyways. I decided to take a bus home rather than the train and I went over to the Port Authority. I bought my ticket and the buses run every hour and I had just missed one so I went out to the street. I wanted to say no to myself, but I couldn't and I didn't put up much of a fight, so I headed over to the peep shows. I passed by Show World, I figured I'd try something new, and one block up on Forty-third I went into a movie theater called The Venus. I paid six bucks to an old, bald man smoking cigarettes and I went inside. The theater was narrow and dark and the floor slanted downward to the screen. The seats were packed tight together and the movie was playing and the projector gave off the only light. I could make out a few scattered men in the rows and one or two shadows along the wall that were men too. I took a seat not near anybody and I watched the three women on the screen who were still dressed talk about sex. I had been in there about two minutes when a guy brushed across my knees to pass me and sat down right next to me. He watched the movie for a minute or two and my heart was racing and then he whispered, "I want to blow you." And I said no, so he said, "Let me touch you then," and I thought about it for a second and I said yes. He started rubbing the inside of my leg with his hand and then he put his palm over my crotch. On the screen the women had their clothes off now and they were positioned all over one another and there were occasional close-ups of tongues going in pussies. The man undid my fly and I gave him a quick look and he had a dark mustache and in that light his skin was shiny, and I thought that probably at one time in his life he had bad acne. He got my penis out and he was stroking me up and down and he started breathing hard and none of the other guys in the theater turned around or looked. In the movie a delivery boy showed up and the women undressed him and tied him up and then the man asked me if I'd go upstairs with him to the bathroom where we could be more private and I said yes. I zipped up my pants and in the corner of the theater was a red sign that said RESTROOM and we went up a little flight of stairs.

The bathroom was dark, the light was out, and we went into a stall with a bench and there was no toilet. I leaned against the wall and the guy undid my pants and he asked me again if he could blow me and I said no. So he started jerking me and then a hand came through the hole in the wall, all these places have holes, and it grabbed my ass, and I moved away, it surprised me, and my guy punched the wall and said, "Fuck off!" And he kept stroking me and asking me to let him blow me and I wouldn't let him, I didn't want his mouth on my dick, and then I came, it just leaked out of me and he felt it on his hand. He said, "That's it?" and he looked at me and he walked out of the stall and he said, "You're a joke," and he went back to the theater. I put my penis back in my pants and I got a little sperm on my fingers. I looked in the bathroom but there was no toilet paper or towels and I didn't want to wipe it on the wall, so I lifted up my pants leg, it was a great idea, and I wiped it on my socks, no one would notice it there. I got out of the theater and I was surprised to see daylight, it was so dark inside, and I ran back to the Port Authority and I got my bus and I slept most of the ride home.

It dropped me off at a gas station a half mile from my house and I could have called and gotten picked up but I decided to walk. I came to my street and it was quiet, and dark, and I went on to the field and walked in the grass and stepped on second base which I always do, it would be bad luck not to. Then I walked to the end of the field and up the slope to the little strip of land that divides the big lake from the little lake. I took the path to the bridge over the waterfall and I stood there and I watched and listened to it pour down and I was glad that the water still wanted to do that. Then I looked back across the big lake, and the trees stirred, there were no leaves, and my eyes ran past Ethan's dock and backyard, and rested there a second, I wondered, where is he? and then my eyes went on down to my house and the yellow porch light was on for me. It was too far to see inside, but I knew that my mother would have the table set beautifully. On Friday nights she makes a big Shabbos meal and when I'm home my father and I wear yarmulkes and he says a prayer over the bread and wine. They were waiting for me and I was thrilled that I could stand there and they didn't know where I was, I could walk all over my own neighborhood and they would never know that I was home. I thought of creeping around my own house and looking in the window, what do they do when I'm not there, what sick things would I see? I stared at my house, at its familiar shape, at everything I know and I realized that I didn't want to see my parents at all. But there was a part of me that wanted to run there as fast as I could and tell them everything and have them hold me, but I couldn't do it, I don't want them to know me. So I thought of just sitting on the bench by the little lake, that's all I would need, but I felt bad for my mother waiting with her dinner and so I ran back to the gas station and went into the phone booth and called.

She answered the phone and I said that I was still in New York and that I was sick with a sore throat and that I was sorry to call so late, but up until the last second I thought I'd come, but I just was feeling too ill. And she was disappointed, but she was understanding and loving too and it felt good to at least tell her a white lie. Then my father picked up another phone and she told him I was sick and that I wouldn't be coming home. And he never lets anybody be sick by themselves and he said, "My left eye has been giving me problems," and I said, "Oh, really," but he didn't bother me. She told me to take care of myself and if I could I should pick up some matzoh because Passover was coming soon and I said I would and then we all started saying our goodbyes. I mumbled something and he said, "Goodnight, son," and she said, "I love you," and I listened and then we all hung up.

I crossed the road from the gas station and I hid behind the bus stop in case my father should go driving by or if someone they knew should see me. After a while when the bus came I jumped out and flagged it down. I sat by the window and I left my street and I didn't think I could ever tell them and I wondered what I would do if and when I became sick. But I put that out of my mind and I told myself that if I'm alive right now, then I'm alive forever. I pushed my seat back as far as it could go and I looked out the window to the dark road. I thought of my parents eating their Friday night dinner and I thought of my father wearing his yarmulke. I sort of wished that I had a yarmulke to wear in the bus.

I HADN'T SEEN Jimmy Warren in a while, so I asked another bum how Jimmy was doing. He said, "You mean Warren the fighter?"

"Yeah, Jimmy Warren. A little guy. Is he all right?"

"Yeah he's all right, he's still taking his next drink."

Then a few days later I spotted Jimmy and I watched him sit calm on a bench and flip open his bottle with his one good thumb. I went up to him and I said hello, but he was too far gone to recognize me. I said to him, "Jimmy, why don't you stop drinking?" And he didn't know who I was, but he heard me and he said, "I guess I'm not ready."

So Jimmy's making it for now, but I know that the bums are dying off. There are more homeless than ever, but the Bowery bum, the white, blue-collar alcoholic, who served in World War II or Korea, is going extinct. The ones that are left, the Jimmy Warren's, the J. B. Britten's, have little orange hospital tags on their wrists; they are like marked precious birds in a sanctuary. But one by one they'll die in some street, or park, or subway tunnel, and the workers, whom I never see, will pick them up and I can't go to their funerals. The bums I've known will be buried somewhere between Manhattan and Long Island and the orange name tags will be taken off their wrists and some piece of paper in some file somewhere will be thrown away.

160

THE CLINIC

I went to the clinic to get my results. I waited
with the black mothers and their children, and with
the gay men and their lovers. The children seemed
healthy, they were noisy and running around and their
mothers were too busy filling out forms to yell at
them. I wanted to call some of the wild ones over
and play with them to pass the time, but I didn't
think it would be right. So I watched people come
out of the swinging doors next to the nurse's desk
and I wondered what they had been told. Unless they
broke into a big smile it was hard to know if they
had been given good news or bad news. After a while
a nurse called my number and she led me down one
long hall and then another till we came to an empty
room with a table and two chairs. We sat down and
she was middle-aged and kind and said that she was
sorry that we had to walk so far, but all the other
rooms were being used. She opened my folder and I

waited and she looked up at me and smiled. She said that my test had come back negative, that I hadn't been exposed to the disease. I looked at her and I knew that it was very important to behave and I said thank you. She showed me the paper and pointed to where the word negative had been stamped, a little crooked, in black ink at the bottom of the page. She offered to make me a copy, so I'd have my own record, and I said I'd like one very much.

She left the room and I took out my wallet and looked at the different things I keep in there. She wasn't gone very long and when she came back I took the copy she made, folded it, and put it next to some money in the billfold. I thanked her again and she wanted to know if I had any questions and I said I had none. So we shook hands and she led me back down the halls to the waiting room. I went through the swinging doors and I walked past the mothers and children and quiet men and no one looked at me. But I wanted someone to notice. I wondered where the person was who had taken my place, who wanted to know what news people had been told. I'm always looking for the person who replaces me, who thinks the things I do, who fills in for me when I'm not there. I know there is someone younger than me doing what I did and someone older doing what I will do, and someone my age being just like me. If he was there in the waiting room I would have told him that I didn't have the disease, but that I needed it. I scanned the chairs for him, but I didn't see him. I figured he'd be there later.

I went outside, it was cool and had become night, and I started walking away from the clinic. I swore to myself that I'd never have to go back there again. But even as I said it I knew how weak my promise was and with each step I took away I felt myself helplessly returning there again and again until I got it right.

I WAS LYING next to Joy and I wanted to kill her because I could hear her swallow. I hated the little thing that was her, that she had to do to live. Then I felt something cold on my hip and I shivered with revulsion, because I'd fallen asleep and then woken up and remembered what we'd just done. I had been lost in the warm blankets and the sounds of the street outside, but then I heard her swallow and then I felt the liquid and I knew we had these horrible bodies with holes and fluids and I was hating myself. I was lying next to her, thirty-four years of emotions and memories and thoughts, and I wanted to pretend she wasn't there because I couldn't love her. And I'm writing this in the nude, I got her to leave, and I can smell my dick and I want to die. I said to her, "I never want to see you again, I want to pretend I've never met you," and she started crying. And I'm getting more ill right now because my fingers hold the pen and my fingers smell and I am losing my mind. She wouldn't stop crying and I wanted to tell her so I did, "I hate to hear you breathe, I hate to hear you swallow."

And it's so horrible, is she just a cunt, I don't want to think that, but that's all I've wanted of her, I wouldn't even kiss her. But I feel so guilty, so terribly guilty, and before she left I asked for forgive-

ness and she screamed at me, "Why are you reject-
ing my love, is it so meaningless to you?" And I didn't
answer, I just let her go, but it is meaningless to me
and I wish I could erase you because I never wanted
to hurt you.

POPPY

I loved my Grandfather. I wear his clothing, it makes me feel close to him. I think when I wear his hat that I will be safe and so I talk to him and say, "Thanks for watching over me Poppy." And the bums on the street ask, "Where'd you get the hat, Red?" So I answer with pride, "It's my Grandfather's." And they smile and seem to understand. When I eat somewhere and I am wearing his clothes I order food that he would like. I used to love to watch him eat, eggs and whitefish at the corners of his mouth, whole rolls shoved in his cheeks, bursting. When he came to visit I would run as fast as I could to hug his big warm belly and he would say with my face pressed tight in his shirt, "Don't run you'll fall." And I would kiss my Poppy on the cheek and he would kiss me back wet on the ear. He was a sad man though and I would ask, "Don't you love Nanny? Why don't you kiss her?" She persecuted him their last years together and his head began to shake and he would write long letters to my family punctuated with the sad phrase, "And on we go."

When I go to his home, dusty now because my Grandmother has lost her mind since he died, I sit in his chair and wait for him to come. I read the old magazines with their old news, and I look at his name on the address labels. But after a while he's not there and so I go to the basement which hasn't changed, and I touch his tools and find little treasures, a watch he's repairing and some old coins, but I don't take any. I'm leaving them there for him and for me, for the next time I come.

I don't know why I wrote those other things about him, I prayed for him to live. I did Poppy, I wore your hat today, I didn't want you to die.

About the Author

Jonathan Ames grew up in New Jersey and graduated from Princeton University in 1987. He is the winner of a Henfield/Transatlantic Review award. He lives in New Jersey.

VINTAGE
CONTEMPORARIES

___ **The Mezzanine** by Nicholson Baker	$7.95	679-72576-8
___ **I Pass Like Night** by Jonathan Ames	$8.95	679-72857-0
___ **Love Always** by Ann Beattie	$5.95	394-74418-7
___ **The History of Luminous Motion** by Scott Bradfield	$8.95	679-72943-7
___ **First Love and Other Sorrows** by Harold Brodkey	$7.95	679-72075-8
___ **Stories in an Almost Classical Mode** by Harold Brodkey	$12.95	679-72431-1
___ **The Debut** by Anita Brookner	$6.95	679-72712-4
___ **Latecomers** by Anita Brookner	$8.95	679-72668-3
___ **Sleeping in Flame** by Jonathan Carroll	$8.95	679-72777-9
___ **Cathedral** by Raymond Carver	$7.95	679-72369-2
___ **Fires** by Raymond Carver	$7.95	679-72239-4
___ **What We Talk About When We Talk About Love** by Raymond Carver	$6.95	679-72305-6
___ **Where I'm Calling From** by Raymond Carver	$8.95	679-72231-9
___ **I Look Divine** by Christopher Coe	$5.95	394-75995-8
___ **Dancing Bear** by James Crumley	$6.95	394-72576-X
___ **The Last Good Kiss** by James Crumley	$6.95	394-75989-3
___ **One to Count Cadence** by James Crumley	$5.95	394-73559-5
___ **The Wrong Case** by James Crumley	$5.95	394-73558-7
___ **The Colorist** by Susan Daitch	$7.95	679-72492-3
___ **The Last Election** by Pete Davies	$6.95	394-74702-X
___ **Great Jones Street** by Don DeLillo	$7.95	679-72303-X
___ **The Names** by Don DeLillo	$7.95	679-72295-5
___ **Players** by Don DeLillo	$7.95	679-72293-9
___ **Ratner's Star** by Don DeLillo	$8.95	679-72292-0
___ **Running Dog** by Don DeLillo	$7.95	679-72294-7
___ **The Commitments** by Roddy Doyle	$6.95	679-72174-6
___ **Selected Stories** by Andre Dubus	$10.95	679-72533-4
___ **From Rockaway** by Jill Eisenstadt	$6.95	394-75761-0
___ **Platitudes** by Trey Ellis	$6.95	394-75439-5
___ **Days Between Stations** by Steve Erickson	$6.95	394-74685-6
___ **Rubicon Beach** by Steve Erickson	$6.95	394-75513-8
___ **A Fan's Notes** by Frederick Exley	$7.95	679-72076-6

VINTAGE
CONTEMPORARIES

___ **Last Notes from Home** by Frederick Exley	$8.95	679-72456-7
___ **Pages from a Cold Island** by Frederick Exley	$6.95	394-75977-X
___ **A Piece of My Heart** by Richard Ford	$6.95	394-72914-5
___ **Rock Springs** by Richard Ford	$6.95	394-75700-9
___ **The Sportswriter** by Richard Ford	$6.95	394-74325-3
___ **The Ultimate Good Luck** by Richard Ford	$5.95	394-75089-6
___ **Bad Behavior** by Mary Gaitskill	$7.95	679-72327-7
___ **Fat City** by Leonard Gardner	$6.95	394-74316-4
___ **Ellen Foster** by Kaye Gibbons	$7.95	679-72866-X
___ **A Virtuous Woman** by Kaye Gibbons	$8.95	679-72844-9
___ **The Late-Summer Passion of a Woman of Mind** by Rebecca Goldstein	$8.95	679-72823-6
___ **We Find Ourselves in Moontown** by Jay Gummerman	$8.95	679-72430-3
___ **Airships** by Barry Hannah	$5.95	394-72913-7
___ **The Cockroaches of Stay More** by Donald Harington	$8.95	679-72808-2
___ **Saigon, Illinois** by Paul Hoover	$6.95	394-75849-8
___ **Angels** by Denis Johnson	$7.95	394-75987-7
___ **Fiskadoro** by Denis Johnson	$6.95	394-74367-9
___ **The Stars at Noon** by Denis Johnson	$5.95	394-75427-1
___ **Asa, as I Knew Him** by Susanna Kaysen	$4.95	394-74985-5
___ **Lulu Incognito** by Raymond Kennedy	$7.95	394-75641-X
___ **Steps** by Jerzy Kosinski	$5.95	394-75716-5
___ **A Handbook for Visitors From Outer Space** by Kathryn Kramer	$5.95	394-72989-7
___ **The Garden State** by Gary Krist	$7.95	679-72515-6
___ **House of Heroes and Other Stories** by Mary La Chapelle	$7.95	679-72457-5
___ **The Chosen Place, the Timeless People** by Paule Marshall	$9.95	394-72633-2
___ **A Recent Martyr** by Valerie Martin	$7.95	679-72158-4
___ **The Consolation of Nature and Other Stories** by Valerie Martin	$6.95	679-72159-2
___ **The Beginning of Sorrows** by David Martin	$7.95	679-72459-1
___ **Suttree** by Cormac McCarthy	$6.95	394-74145-5
___ **California Bloodstock** by Terry McDonell	$8.95	679-72168-1

VINTAGE
CONTEMPORARIES

___ **The Bushwhacked Piano** by Thomas McGuane	$7.95	394-72642-1
___ **Nobody's Angel** by Thomas McGuane	$7.95	394-74738-0
___ **Something to Be Desired** by Thomas McGuane	$4.95	394-73156-5
___ **To Skin a Cat** by Thomas McGuane	$5.95	394-75521-9
___ **Bright Lights, Big City** by Jay McInerney	$5.95	394-72641-3
___ **Ransom** by Jay McInerney	$5.95	394-74118-8
___ **Story of My Life** by Jay McInerney	$6.95	679-72257-2
___ **Mama Day** by Gloria Naylor	$8.95	679-72181-9
___ **The All-Girl Football Team** by Lewis Nordan	$5.95	394-75701-7
___ **Welcome to the Arrow-Catcher Fair** by Lewis Nordan	$6.95	679-72164-9
___ **River Dogs** by Robert Olmstead	$6.95	394-74684-8
___ **Soft Water** by Robert Olmstead	$6.95	394-75752-1
___ **Family Resemblances** by Lowry Pei	$6.95	394-75528-6
___ **Sirens** by Steve Pett	$8.95	394-75712-2
___ **Clea & Zeus Divorce** by Emily Prager	$6.95	394-75591-X
___ **A Visit From the Footbinder** by Emily Prager	$6.95	394-75592-8
___ **Mohawk** by Richard Russo	$8.95	679-72577-6
___ **The Risk Pool** by Richard Russo	$8.95	679-72334-X
___ **Rabbit Boss** by Thomas Sanchez	$8.95	679-72621-7
___ **Anywhere But Here** by Mona Simpson	$7.95	394-75559-6
___ **Carnival for the Gods** by Gladys Swan	$6.95	394-74330-X
___ **The Player** by Michael Tolkin	$7.95	679-72254-8
___ **Myra Breckinridge and Myron** by Gore Vidal	$8.95	394-75444-1
___ **The Car Thief** by Theodore Weesner	$6.95	394-74097-1
___ **Breaking and Entering** by Joy Williams	$6.95	394-75773-4
___ **Taking Care** by Joy Williams	$5.95	394-72912-9
___ **The Easter Parade** by Richard Yates	$8.95	679-72230-0
___ **Eleven Kinds of Loneliness** by Richard Yates	$8.95	679-72221-1
___ **Revolutionary Road** by Richard Yates	$8.95	679-72191-6

Now at your bookstore or call toll-free to order: 1-800-733-3000
(credit cards only).